I0667547

I've just read A HOME IN THE MIST: THE STRANGER by W.T. Ridenour. I was amazed at the knowledge of the author as he writes about the birds, plants, and the geology of the area. I sat spellbound as I read this book written about Cade's Cove and the hardships encountered by these mountain people. I admired the way they helped one another in times of trouble as well as the determination to make a life for themselves and their families under difficult circumstances. I'm looking forward to the sequel and hope there will be many more such books from this author.

Darlene Jackson

THE FIRST BOOK IN . . .

A HOME IN THE MIST SERIES: THE STRANGER. NEEDS TO BE A MOTION PICTURE:

Yes, Mark Twain knew the Mississippi, but this gentleman knows Cade's Cove and how to spin a great novel! When's the last time you shared a book with your husband and wanted to read it to your grandkids? This one is it! It truly needs to be picked up by a major publishing house . . .

I am not for sure where Mr. Ridenour has been hiding all his life, but hopefully he will be spending the rest of it with pen in hand or his computer keys clicking! I can only guess he has spent many days outdoors with wildlife, campfires, and grand stories spinning in his head. I, for one, am thankful he finally decided to share. He definitely has a fan base building.

Candace Hickman

A HOME IN THE MIST II

A CADES COVE STORY

DIVER'S STORY

W.T. RIDENOUR

Author photo © 2020 by Kathy J. Ridenour.

Cover photo © by Pixabay.

Cover design © 2020 by Timothy M. Ridenour.

Edited and formatted by Cherel S. Justice.

Published by William T. Ridenour.

ISBN 978-1-7358587-2-2 (paperback)
ISBN 978-1-7358587-3-9 (ebook)

TO KATHY

Table of Contents

Prologue

WELCOME BACK. DON'T KNOW ABOUT y'all but I'm feeling a heap better after stretching out these old legs of mine. Got my chores done too, so the missus is happy. What she don't know is them chores didn't take half the time she thinks they did.

Shoo doggy, I been out here on the porch for quite a spell now eatin' me some good ol' buttered cornbread soaked in a bowl of cold buttermilk. As for you young'uns that ain't never tried it; why, y'all don't know what you been a-missin'. That's some real fine eatin' there.

Oh well, forgive an old man's rambling. I reckon y'all came back to hear some more about the Cove story.

Let's see now. Seems to me we left off when Diver had just got me and Henry down off that cliff we were stuck on and we had ourselves a real fine reunion. Pa, as you can imagine, was over the moon that he was taking us home. He hugged us both, then held us out at arms length to see if we were injured and hugged us again. Then, he threatened to tan out hides if we ever put him and Ma through such a thing again.

All in all, it was a mighty fine reunion.

By the time we made it to Abrams Creek, Clarence and his boys were just coming down the last of that slope opposite from where they spotted Henry and me. We all met up at the confluence of the streams. Of course, there was another grand reunion. Pa 'bout beat poor Clarence half to death thankin' him for finding me and Henry. Can't say it did the man's enjured leg a lot o' good, but Pa sure was happy.

Then, against Clarence's wishes, Pa ordered Dean and Pat to help him get Clarence on his back and he carried him to the wagon. It took forty-five minutes, but Pa made it look like he was carrying no more than a basket of eggs.

When we reached the wagon, everyone made a fuss over makin' sure Clarence was as comfortable as possible. He kept sayin' he was just fine, but we paid him no mind until he finally shouted, "Get your cotton-pickin' hands off o' me." That 'bout got everyone tickled and we burst out laughin' so hard it even got ol' Clarence to chucklin'. We all piled in around him and had a mighty fine time on the ride home.

Dean dropped Pa, Diver, me, and Henry off at the base of our Cove trail to spare Clarence the extra jostling that old track up the ridge would've given him.

After a last round of heartfelt thanks and fond farewells, we set our sights for home.

We were dirty, tired, ragged, and hungry . . . and four of the happiest chaps you'd ever want to meet in your life.

ONE

Home

WHEN ME AND HENRY WALKED into the cabin and I saw Ma, I felt about as low as a person could get. Now don't get me wrong I was plumb thankful to be home and all, and the look on Ma's face was somethin' to behold. She lit up and shined like that big ol' ray a sunlight I once saw reflecting off o' Mable Davis' duck pond.

But behind that big ol' glowin' smile, I could see the toll this ordeal had taken on her. In just two days it looked like she had aged ten years.

Long Star had paid a price too, I reckon, but being younger and living every day exposed to the harshness of a lonely wilderness life she just naturally had a better coping mechanism. I think her inner sight refused to let her believe we were dead without proof, thereby saving her from sinking to the depths of the sorrow that Ma had reached.

Anyway, Henry and me just stood around and let everybody take their turn patting, and pawing, and smiling, and kissing, and carrying on in every way they could think of to make a twelve-year-old boy plumb uncomfortable.

After that, they started in on how brave and strong we were, and how proud they were to know such fine upstanding young men, and how we were a true asset to the community. You know, all that highfalutin praise that a body somehow earns by gettin' through a situation that they never wanted to be in, in the first place.

Why, by the time they were done, I 'bout had tears in my own eyes just considerin' what amazing boys me and Henry were.

And to think all of this was because we had gone and got ourselves lost. Can't say I really understood the reasoning there.

From how I heard it later, the Tudwells had also taken 'bout all the praise they could handle for findin' us.

Seems it somehow got out that we had been found, and that Clarence had risked his life and nearly died rescuing us. The story spread about how he had been critically injured savin' me and Henry from certain death, and but for the Lord's good graces may not pull through.

Exactly how that rumor spread, I don't know; but seein's how only us and Clarence's boys even knew we had been found, I reckon one of them boys must have been the source.

"They's lookin' to find their long-widowed Pa a new wife," Ma suggested.

If that was the intent, it sure could have played out if Clarence had been willing. Rolf later told Pa he figured every single woman over eighteen years old in the whole Cove showed up to fawn over ol' Clarence.

It was a well-intentioned circle of womenfolk traipsing around the poor man's house with all their handshakin', backslappin', and come-to-supper-next-Sundayin'. Of course, Clarence had no choice but to allow the two or three 'take charge' ladies to clean and dress his wounds and make sure he was all comfy and whatnot. They applied a heavy cream made of aloe, plantain, and honey, that Clarence had to admit did ease the pain some, and they assured him it would speed up the healing too.

Finally, when the gals all gathered in the kitchen to fix supper, Clarence saw his chance and made Dean and Pat help him sneak out the backway and hide in the barn. He told the boys if either of 'em gave up his refuge to one of them pesky women he'd give 'em a switchin' like they'd never seen before.

Pat laughed and said they weren't kids no more, but when he got a look at his pa's stink-eye he decided he may not be as growed up as he thought.

While all that was going on down at the Tudwell farm, Pa and Diver was at our place dragging a mess of logs and green brush out into the pasture to light as a signal fire. The bellowing smoke from the green-wood fire was to signal the various search parties to come on in. The search was over.

As it was gettin' late, some of the search parties were already on their way in, but the signal caught the attention of some others. By full dark all but two parties were accounted for and with cheers of joy upon discovering we had been found, and heartfelt thanks from our families, they harnessed up their various forms of conveyance and headed home.

Hester Wo, the blind, old shoemaker, had helped Sarah May around the kitchen. She said he had been a surprisingly delightful conversationalist. He shared many tales of growing up as a cobbler's son in the city of Philadelphia. When his ride pulled up out front, he tipped his cap, bid her a fond farewell, and said hoped they'd get a chance to speak again. She told him they surely would and gave him a little hug before he bundled into the squeaky-wheeled buckboard with his friends and started down the trail to the Cove.

By that time, it was getting on to full dark and only two search parties were still missing, Pa knew the men in the two parties who were still out and figured they would bed down overnight and continue the search in the morning. He'd head out early and bring 'em in.

Forrest, who had returned shortly before dark, helped Diver do the evening chores. Me and Henry had offered to help, but our job was to stay near our mas to reassure them we was okay.

Bits and pieces of our ordeal had come out over the course of the evening, but no one had gotten a complete picture of what happened. So, it was agreed that after supper, when everyone could gather around, we would tell the complete tale.

When the time came, the kids were sent to the loft for fear the story might be too frightful for young ears. But they were too quiet up there, so I was sure they were listenin' through the ceiling. When the adults were all settled in with fresh cups o' coffee, I reckon that was about the biggest audience that kitchen ever saw.

As for me and Henry, we stood there by the fireplace and rather hesitantly at first, began to tell the tale. Well, I guess the truth is, I began telling the tale. Henry was a bit more reserved in front of all my kinfolk and only spoke up to clarify a point now and then.

It didn't take long, what with all them folks hanging on my every word, before I started really getting into it. Looking back, I can see as where a point here and there may have come out a bit more dramatic than it actually happened. But overall, I figure we gave a fairly accurate account.

"It all started," I began, "when me and Henry decided to spend the night in a cave."

From there I mentioned our ghost stories and waking up to see glowing eyes. I told about Henry's brave stand against the beast and how we escaped down the crawl. I didn't mention Henry's previous, near fatal experience in the crawl. That would remain between us.

When I described how we had to lay on our sides to pull and push ourselves along with our fingertips and toes, I saw a few faces go pale in the glow of our coal oil lanterns. I then played out Henry being stuck in the hole in the ceiling at the end of the crawl; and how I pushed and pulled, trying to find out what he was caught on; all the while thinking the panther was surely coming.

With everyone in the kitchen holdin' their breath as if to help Henry squeeze through the bind, I caused a sudden burst of laughter describing how the moment he was loose, I nearly crawled over his back to get to the room above.

But they all settled down in a hurry when I told of the battle between Henry and the beast, and how my smashing it on the head with a large rock was pure luck.

At that point, Pa and Diver glanced at each other, finally understanding how the cat had come by his facial injuries.

After that, I described our long, cold, exhausting ordeal through the cavernous silence in pitch darkness. Told 'em how we finally found water, only to have it become a wall-to-wall stream, and finally a water chute.

I saw a look of shock and fear on their faces when I related our decision to slide down the dark water chute not knowing where it went. It very well may've plunged us into an underground tube with no air at all, where we would have drowned and floated forever in a midnight world of silent nothingness. I tried to explain to them that we really had no choice, but only seeing startled gazes, I quickly moved on.

I described the midstream column of rock that saved both of our lives. Then I told 'em of the loss of our last light source and how we passed out from utter exhaustion.

I explained how I woke-up, not realizing at first that I could see. And how we were only ten feet or so from the cave's exit.

Lastly and with great fanfare, I placed a gold Spanish escudo on the kitchen table. To a startled chorus of oohs and aahs, I described finding the skeleton of Moss Zeekman and how Henry found the initials 'MZ' carved into the handle of his old rusty knife. After that, Henry, and I both emptied our pockets and shoes and stacked sixteen coins on the table to be examined and admired.

While everyone was excitedly looking over the loot, I motioned for Pa to follow me and we slipped out into the front yard.

"Pa," I said, "I been thinking 'bout that gold."

Pa just stood there with folded arms and nodded for me to continue.

"I'd like to give you and Ma each a gold piece and give one to Forrest. I'd like you to save one for Delma too. Then I figured I'd keep one for myself and give one to Diver."

Pa continued to nod.

"That's six. The other ten, I'd like to give to Henry. He's the only reason we got out of that cave and I think he deserves the lion's share."

Pa laid his big hand on my shoulder. "I think that's about as fine an idea as I've ever heard."

I believe I may've seen a bit of moisture in his eyes. It was hard to tell being night and all.

"I'm proud of you, son," he said.

We went back inside, and Pa said I had something to say. I told everybody what I'd told Pa, and they all clapped and cheered and said what a fine idea it was. Henry, of course, tried to downplay his role, saying he didn't deserve it; but it weren't no use. He was the hero, like it or not. And he and Long Star had just become a little richer.

As everyone was congratulating Henry and asking a startled Long Star what they were going to do with their newfound wealth; I happened to glance up and see Diver standing in his favorite place against the back wall. He had a look of pride in his eyes. I nearly choked on the knot that grew in my throat. I can't even explain what that man's approval meant to me.

After a bit, when the excitement had calmed down, Pa took the floor.

"I know everybody is all excited about what happened, and the story is gonna sweep the Cove like wildfire. There's just one thing I'd like to ask. If it gets out that the skeleton of Moss Zeekman has been found, we're gonna have so many treasure hunters and Moss Zeekman Lost Gold Mine scammers flooding into these mountains, it won't be a fit place to live. So, I ask that we all agree right now that we can talk about the boy's adventures all we want, but that no one will mention Moss Zeekman or the gold."

A quick scan of the table confirmed that everyone agreed. We sat there in quiet thought for a moment, hoping what Pa feared would never reach the Cove. Then from the loft above we heard a very loud and distinct whisper.

"I will not. I ain't sayin' nothin' 'bout no Ma Beepman."

We laughed so hard, Sarah May suddenly grabbed her skirts and rushed out the back door—which only made the rest of us laugh harder.

TWO

Church & Checkers

AFTER FORREST'S FAMILY WENT HOME that night, Henry and Long Star took my sleeping loft. I was fine on the reed mat near the kitchen fireplace, and Diver went back to his room in the barn. I would've gone to the barn too, but Pa thought it'd be best if I was available if Ma needed to see me.

The next mornin' Henry helped me do my chores before breakfast. By then Two Hand had shown up somehow knowing we had been found. He, Pa, and Diver, sat out front eating a large breakfast and discussing the search and recovery. Of course, there was also plenty of strong coffee; a treat Two Hand never tired of. Two Hand said he knew where the other two search teams were and he'd send 'em in, saving Pa and Diver the trouble.

After breakfast, Long Star and Henry promised not to be strangers and said their goodbyes. Then Two Hand, after acceptin' a poke of green coffee beans from Pa and a hug from Ma, led them away into the waiting forest.

The next several days were uneventful. I pretty much stayed near home and helped Ma with her garden and the chickens and all. Pa fetched the bedrolls from the cave, so there was no reason for me to go back there. To tell the truth, if he hadn't retrieved 'em, I reckon they would have been left there, 'cause that was one place I had no desire to go.

Diver and Pa spent a great deal of time workin' with the new cornfield and building an irrigation system that Diver had designed. It was quite a brilliant contraption consisting of a series of flumes and gates that allowed a controlled water supply when needed and could be completely shut down when there was plenty of rain. Diver said the slight slope of the field was the key to the entire project 'cause it allowed perfect drainage, preventing the crop from being overwatered.

Come Saturday afternoon, Pa thrilled Ma when he asked Diver to hitch up the mule team and wagon in the mornin'. Said the family was goin' to church. Ma didn't know what to think. In all the years they'd been married, Pa only went to church twice. Once when Forrest married Sarah May and then again when Delma married Jim.

Ma rushed around like a schoolgirl checkin' that our best clothes were all mended and clean. She put water on to boil for baths and tried to do things that in her mind needed to be done, but that me and Pa would've never even considered.

"Oh Zeb," she said, "I wish you'd a given me some warnin'. I don't know what got into you. But don't get me wrong, I'm sure pleased."

She then gave Pa a big ol' hug before rushin' off to continue her preparations.

I could see a kind of melancholy look on Pa's face. He was happy that Ma was so pleased, but he knew he really didn't deserve the credit. He was simply fulfilling a commitment. Diver was the only one that knew about Pa's promise to God and Pa was not one to make promises lightly. But then whatever the reason, Ma was happy and that made Pa happy.

He reached out and squeezed my shoulder. "Go help your ma," he said. "She's looking mighty chipper right now, but with what she's been through, I want you to keep an eye on her."

"Yes sir, I sure will," I said.

He then left the cabin to go talk with Diver.

When Diver had time on Sunday mornings, he'd often walk all the way into the Cove and visit the Cade's Cove Baptist Church. He enjoyed the preaching of Pastor Wilson and the fellowship of Forrest and his family. And when he could, he enjoyed visiting with the Cobbs and many more of the church community he'd come to know since that fateful day that Pa pulled him home on that travois. Now he'd be going to church as part of the Banion Clan. He may not have been bustling around the way Ma was, but he was surely pleased.

Come morning, when we came marchin' into the church and sat down like it weren't nothin' but any other Sunday, I reckon you could've heard an earth worm's belly rumble. Why, Pastor Wilson stood there at the pulpit with wide eyes and a startled look on his face. I think I saw his lips moving for a full twenty seconds before he cleared his throat and sound began comin' out.

"Welcome, welcome," he said. "We're so glad you could join us this fine day."

After that we had a prayer and sang a few songs. Then Pastor Wilson started his announcements by sharing some sad news. Sister Gertrude Crouse, who had been a member in good standing of the Methodist community, had been down with a bad case of the croup for several days. Dr. Kendree was called in. Unfortunately, despite his best ministrations, she worsened and died in the early hours of the morning. Not having any relatives in the Cove, her brother's family in Knoxville was being notified. The funeral was to be held on Tuesday and all who wished to celebrate her long and caring life were welcome. The time and particulars would be posted on community billboards throughout the Cove.

After the announcements we had another prayer, then a real nice sermon about the Good Samaritan and how we should all strive to meet the needs of others the way he did.

After church, Pa, Diver, Forrest, and Pastor Wilson talked for a while, while Ma and Sarah May visited with friends not seen nearly often enough. I was just standin' around watchin' folks load up and leave and wonderin' why Second Chance hadn't showed up with his family, when I heard a soft voice behind me.

"I was mighty glad to hear you came home."

I spun around and my breath caught in my throat. There stood Mary Wilson, looking fine as could be in her Sunday best.

"Hey, Mary," I said, putting both hands in my pockets and shining the tip of my right shoe on the back of my left pant leg. "I's hopin' to see ya here."

Then realizing what I'd just said, I followed up with, "You and Second Chance and all."

"Oh, Second Chance has some friends that go over to the Methodist Church, so his pa lets him go there with his Uncle Tod and his family."

And right then, when she had me off my guard and I wasn't suspectin' a thing, she did it again. With that slight tilt of her head, which caught my attention, she peeked up at me outta the corner of her eye and softly said, "I was kinda hoping you might be wanting to see me."

I like to of come undone right then and there.

"I, I, I did," I stammered. I was so frazzled I really didn't know what I was sayin'.

Luckily, it was right then that Pa shouted out, "Come on, Billy, we're leaving."

I didn't know what to think. I hated to leave Mary, and at the same time I was so flustered I couldn't wait to get away from her.

"I gotta go," I said, as I turned to leave.

Behind me I heard a sweet, drawn-out, "B-y-e, Billy." Now I ain't swearin' to it or nothin', but I think I heard a giggle. I'm not sure, 'cause I didn't look back. I kinda felt like my face was sunburned and I was standing in a bucket of ice water; all at the same time.

As I climbed aboard the wagon, Pa and Diver didn't take notice, but Ma had a poorly concealed grin on her face. When we pulled out of the churchyard, she took hold of Pa's upper arm with both her hands and laid her head against his shoulder. He sat up a little straighter, and there may've been just a hint of color flushin' his cheek too. Yeah, that sunburn seemed to be spreadin' on the Banion menfolk that day.

All in all, it was a real fine Sunday.

Other than just goin' to church, another sudden change in Pa's routine was he began makin' the occasional trip down the hill to check on Clarence. They were fast becoming true friends and valued neighbors.

It was on one of those visits that Clarence introduced Pa to the game of checkers. Pa was so taken with it, he spent the best part of a Sunday afternoon crafting his own set and then he patiently taught Ma, Diver, and me how to play. Many a night after supper, the table was cleared and out came the board. There was laughter and jokes, stories and tall tales, and everyone strived to be declared king or queen of the board for that night. Though to tell the truth, on occasion I saw Diver make uncharacteristic bad moves that cost him the game.

I don't think Ma or Pa ever realized what was happening. They always had a foot stompin', table slappin' good time with lots of laughter at Diver's expense. He just joined in, shaking his head as if in disbelief at such a silly move, and ended up bein' the one laughing the loudest of all.

Those were some happy days, but in this life there's always a poke of sadness waitin' 'round the corner. The first to come our way was news Forrest brought up from the Cove while deliverin' a load of sugar, coffee, flour, and a letter from Delma.

"Heard a bit more about Mrs. Crouse," he said. "Come to find out, when old Mrs. Crouse had the croup and Doc Kendree visited her, he once again prescribed bleeding as the best treatment. He did his thing and asked her closest neighbor to check in on her in the mornin' and fix her a good breakfast to get her strength up. He didn't even deem it worthwhile to check back on her himself.

He continued that it turned out, during the night, whether 'cause she laid wrong, or the bandage slipped, or just 'cause she was an old woman with frail arms and weak blood vessels; the vein which Kendree slit for the bleedin' reopened. Not a lot the poor ol' gal could've done about it, bein' along and all as she was. Even if she'd been awake and aware of it; which is doubtful, there was no evidence that she tried to staunch the flow.

As it turned out, long before morning her life's blood had drained out onto the worn, pinewood floor of her well-tended home.

When word reached Knoxville about Gertrude's true cause of death, rumor spread that three of her nephews were on their way to tar and feather Kendree and ride him out of town on a rail. It's doubtful any of the Cove folk would have tried to stop 'em either.

Pa offered that a few of them may've even joined in.

But the morning after the rumor started, Kendree up and disappeared. I reckon he'd come to see the Cove as a 'not so healthy' place to live. It's said he was in such a hurry he up and left most of his belongings and just vanished.

As it turns out, the Crouse boys never showed. But I don't reckon anyone was all that anxious to hunt down the doctor and invite him back.

For quite a spell after that professional medical care in the Cove was limited. There was the mid-wife, Mable Davis, whom Pa had a high regard for; Josh

Custer, the veterinarian, who was a bit on the rough side, but came in handy for settin' a bone or removin' an ornery splinter, and Buck Wadsworth, the barber-surgeon-dentist.

The thing about Buck was, and he'd tell you himself, he knew nothing at all about medicine. The way he saw it, medicine was for "healing it so you could keep it." A barber-surgeon-dentist's job was to "gettin' rid of it."

"Weren't no medicine involved," he said.

If those three couldn't manage your ailment and you had the means to make the trip, Doc Hickman, over in Sevierville, was mighty highly thought of. And not once in his many years of practice had he bought into the bleeding theory.

THREE

Champion Pig Catcher

IN THE COVE, ORWELL BECKETT was the biggest promoter of the Independence Day celebration. As a young man he had served in the War for Independence with distinction under Horatio Gates during the disastrous defeat at Camden, and later received praise from Gen. Nathanael Greene himself in one of the most successful campaigns of the war against Britain's 'Southern Strategy.'

Every year on July 4th, he threw a party for the entire Cove. There were competitions in rail splitting, greased pig catching, foot races, cow milking, and pie eating. Judges gave prizes for the best: pies, cakes, pickles, jams, moonshine; and the fattest hog. Though betting was discouraged, plenty of money changed hands during the horse races, trick shooting competition, wrestling, turkey shoots, and axe throwing demonstrations.

As evening drew near, there was a huge picnic with several roasted pigs and half a beef cow on an enormous rotating grill, all supplied by Orwell. Along with the roasted meats, the church ladies served a whole plethora of both wild and garden greens. And of course, everyone's favorite, the best baked goods in the mountains.

To drink, there was sassafras tea, spruce tea, milk, beer, six types of wine and several flavors of grain or fruit-based moonshine.

Finally, with full dark closing in, the well-fed crowd gathered 'round Orwell's five-acre stock pond and oohed and aahed as fireworks burst in the sky. Red, white, and blue fireworks were added to the more common orange ones, making the spectacle even more magnificent.

Ma had invited Long Star and Henry to join us, so Forrest picked up Ma, Pa and Long Star in Orwell's carriage and me, Henry and Diver were to follow in Pa's wagon. After Orwell's carriage left, Diver had me and Henry help him load Pa's biggest and laziest hog in the wagon, and we were on our way.

It was quite a day and other than a spat between Forrest and Trace Beckett, everyone had a great time.

Forrest, being the champion wrestler from the previous year, only had to face two top contenders from the day's bouts. Trace, thinking mighty highly of himself threw his hat in the ring and easily took a top contender's spot, but when he faced Forrest, he went down three falls to nothing. Furious and embarrassed, he snatched up a barrel stave used by the cooks to move the roasted pigs off the spit and attacked Forrest with it. Trace's pa, Jud, started to step in and help his son, but Pa stopped him with a rifle barrel poke to the belly. Forrest allowed Trace one swing with the stave and as it swished by, he stepped in and laid his opponent out. Trace suddenly became too busy nappin' to give it a second try. Pa lowered his rifle and turned to Orwell, who had witnessed the whole thing.

"We good?" asked Pa.

"I ain't seen a thing but friendly competition," said Orwell. "And my foreman won."

Pa smiled and laid his extra-large hand on Orwell's skinny shoulder. "That's what I saw," he said, "but if you got a minute, there's something I need to discuss with ya."

Orwell nodded and the two men walked off together talkin' like old friends.

Jud was seething as he threw water into his son's face and helped him to a nearby seat, all the while watching the two men. It was all he could do not to lash out, but even he dared not cross his older brother.

While Forrest was the wrestling champ, it was Pa who took the day.

Top prizes included: a new saddle with intricate art work, for horse racing, two pairs of top-quality leather boots for foot racing and wrestlin', four of Jim Bowie's new fighting knives for rail splitting, trick shooting, axe throwing, and the turkey shoot; and one new .54 caliber Hawken's rifle for overall top score of the day.

Scores were tallied at three points for first place, two points for second, and one point for third. Top total score wins the day.

Early in the day, Jud had taken the rail splitting competition by beatin' the Deerborn brothers, Rolf Schmidt, and his own son, Trace. He won a Bowie knife. Then Pa won trick shootin' by dousing three candles without hitting wax at fifty yards. He received the second Bowie knife.

Later in the afternoon, Trace was again disappointed when Charley Wrightman knocked him out of the axe throwing demonstration. He protested that a girl should not be allowed to enter, but the rules were examined, and no such exclusion was found. She could compete. Unfortunately for Charley, it was all for naught. Jud stepped in and won his second Bowie knife of the day by outthrowing her in the final heat.

The Turkey shoot consisted of triangles drawn on a wood plank and placed twenty-five yards from the shooters. The object was to shoot away all three tips of the triangle with the plank being moved twenty-five yards farther out after each shot. The farthest accurate shot would win.

Pa was neck to neck with another mountain man known as Skeeter Bissell who figured he was about "the finest marksman that ever strolled the wilds of the mountains or the wide stretches of the prairies."

Pa won the prize; his second Bowie knife, at a distance of one-hundred-seventy-five yards. It was an amazing feat which was greeted with lots of cheering and congratulations from the onlookers.

Skeeter, on the other hand, was quite perplexed. He just couldn't understand what was wrong with his long gun. It never even occurred to him he could have simply been outshot.

With that being the last competition, it was time for the overall winner to be named and awarded the highly prized, brand new, .54 caliber Hawken rifle.

Manufactured in St Louis, Missouri, it was a show-case model. With a four hundred yard effective range, it was quite likely the single most prized weapon in the mountains.

With much pomp and circumstance, the tally was taken, but an unforeseen problem presented itself. Pa and Jud had each won two major competitions at three points per event. Seldom had anyone taken first place in more than one three-point event, and yet that year there were two double winners. The tally stood at six points each.

A meeting was held between all the judges and Orwell Beckett. An additional competition as a tiebreaker didn't seem advisable lest it play to one or the other's advantage.

Orwell couldn't let it be speculated that he had skewed the competition in his brother's favor. Yet he also knew that Pa would never accept an event that gave him an unfair advantage over Jud.

It was quite a perplexing situation until suddenly, quite out of the blue, a solution was presented to them.

"It's not a tie," said Diver.

Orwell was taken aback by such a statement. He knew Diver had proven himself to be an honest and highly respected man in the community.

"How can you say that two first place wins against two first place wins ain't a tie?" he exclaimed.

"Well ya see," said Diver. "While we were all gathered 'round watchin' the big competitions over here, they were holdin' the hog judging competition back yonder at the stock pins."

Everyone glanced over at Orwell's barns, then back at Diver.

"Tommy Linden just informed me that Zeb's hog took third place in the fattest hog category. That's good for one point. Way I figure it, that gives Zeb seven points overall against Jud's six."

The crowd burst out in laughter and cheering. Men slapped Pa on the back and raised a toast to the champion of the games. Jud was green-eyed and furious but couldn't deny the tally. He'd been beat by a third place hog. He pushed his way through the crowd and stomped over to the moonshine booth, not waiting to see Pa receive his prize.

"Congratulations," said Diver as he held out his open hand.

Pa looked at his friend. "How many times are you gonna pull my bacon out o' the fire?" he said, as he took Diver's proffered hand and shook it.

"Didn't do a thing," said Diver. "Oh sure, I may've entered that hog for ya without coming right out and telling ya, but it was your bacon, so to speak, after all."

Pa laughed, Diver shrugged, and the two friends tried to fend off all the well-wishers. It took some time, but the crowd drifted off to other pursuits. Pa and Diver, loaded down with Pa's Pennsylvania longrifle, the Hawkens, and a new .54 caliber mold set, along with two highly polished Bowie knives, went in search of the womenfolk.

"Here comes Zeb and Diver," Long Star said, as she, Ma, and Sarah May, were just finishing the cleanup of the fourteen-foot-long, oak plank, pie eating table.

"Well they're too late for dessert," said Ma with a smile.

"I don't know," quipped Sarah May as she scrapped several more clumps of scattered fruit and crust into a bucket. "We could just sit 'em down here and let 'em nibble on the tabletop. Save ourselves a ton of work."

Ma laughed, "That may be, but I reckon Orwell would get mighty upset when he saw how somebody had done chewed a hole through his best picnic table."

Sarah May and Long Star laughed.

"What's so funny," asked Pa, as he and Diver strolled up.

"Oh, nothin'," said Ma. "Just girl talk."

The other women just turned away and giggled.

"Whatcha got there?" Ma asked, admiring Pa's new Rifle.

Pa proudly held it out in front of him so Ma could get a better look.

"It's a brand new .54 caliber Hawken," said Pa. "I just won it for having a fat pig."

"A fat pig?" said Ma.

"Yeah, and the critter didn't even have enough pride to be the fattest—he was third fattest."

Ma had a rather confused look on her face. "That's a story I gotta hear," she said.

"I'll tell ya all about it on the way home," Pa promised.

While the adults were busy doin' their thing; me, Henry, and Second Chance, were runnin' around trying to see everything at once. It's not often that a backwoods mountain boy gets to experience anything like Orwell's Independence Day celebration, and we weren't lookin' to miss any of it.

As we dodged around stands, leaped over sittin' stumps, and generally made a nuisance of ourselves, the adult population seemed to ignore us pretty much. It may've had somethin' to do with them knowin' we were the two boys that were lost in the mountains. Or perhaps it was just that they knew whose son I was. Most folks still didn't quite know how to take Pa. Whatever it was, we were havin' a good ol' time.

Then, what do I do but come tearing around the side of a display tent and run smack dab into Mary Wilson.

Well now, anyone who has ever been pleasantly strollin' along mindin' their own business, and then suddenly had someone jump out and land right in their face, knows it's a bit startling. You tend to react before you think. And that's exactly what Mary did.

With a little screech of surprise, Mary jumped straight back without lookin', and landed smack dab center of a big old sleepin' hound dog.

Now, I reckon that old hound dog must've been mighty confused about what infraction he may have broken to bring down such a punishment upon himself, and he sure wasn't lookin' to stick around for any more of it. He jumped up, and with a long, drawn-out howl, he headed for safer grounds. Unfortunately, Mary was still sprawled out on his back with her feet slapping against his floppy ears, and his tail excitedly thumping her right atop her pretty blue bonnet. He must've hauled her a good twenty feet before they finally parted ways. She was left sittin' in a trampled patch of purple alfalfa clove; grass stained, disheveled, and bewildered.

"WHAT are you doing, you big oaf?"

Susan Beckett, Tyrone's little sister and Mary's best friend, stood there with her hands on her hips and stared me straight in the eyes.

I was frozen in place, not knowing what to do, or say. While Susan was a year younger than me, and a full head shorter, right then she was about the scariest sight I could imagine.

"Well, don't just stand there, help her up," she said.

With that my brain reengaged, and I hurried over to Mary and helped her regain her feet.

"I'm so sorry, Mary," I said, as I pulled her to a standing position.

She still had a startled, blank look on her face, as if not knowing what had just happened.

I suppose it would be a bit disconcerning to be walking along one minute and sprawled out the next.

"Are you okay?" I asked.

She came to herself then, and while gingerly brushing the dust off her backside, she looked around to make sure no more hounds were gonna take her for a ride. Finally, she started to smile, and her cheeks reddened to a quite attractive, rosy glow.

"I'm alright, Billy," she said.

"You sure?" I asked.

"Yes, I'm sure," she said, "as the smile spread across her face. "Just a bit embarrassed. That was quite an entrance you made."

"It was a stupid entrance," sneered Susan, still steamed and willing to show it.

"I know, I know," I said.

I was really surprised at the reaction from Susan. She may have been Tyrone's little sister, but she was normally nothin' like the rest of the Becketts. She was usually quiet, respectful, and very friendly. So much so, that even though she was the sister of Mary's arch enemy, she was still Mary's closest friend.

"Now calm down Susan," said Mary. "He didn't mean to do it, and he apologized."

"Yeah, well . . . well." Frustrated, Susan slapped her hands on her sides. "Well if you're willing to forgive him, I guess I'll hafta too."

Then she gave me the stink eye. "But you better watch yourself, bub," she said.

Maybe she was more Beckett than I'd thought.

Turning around, I saw Henry and Second Chance nearly rolling on the ground laughing.

"Ha, ha," I said. I could feel the tips of my ears heatin' up and knew they were gettin' redder by the second. It was embarrassing—especially in front of Mary—but there was nothin' I could do about it.

I do have to give Mary credit though. She didn't say a thing. She simply took me by the arm, nodded toward a refreshment tent and said, "I could sure use some nice, cold sassafras tea."

"Sure," I said. As we headed toward the Cade's Cove Baptist Church tent, I glanced over my shoulder. Henry and Second Chance were still laughin' and smirkin', but they were followin' too. Wasn't a thing I could do about Henry, but I figured Second Chance was gonna be in for a thumpin'.

The five of us spent the rest of the day together enjoyin' the party. Henry, Second Chance, and me, had already been soundly beat in the pie eating contest by some skinny kid from the west end of the Cove. Must've been a new family 'cause I'd never seen him before. So anyway, we figured since we were already a mess, we may as well enter the greased pig competition.

The rules were simple; the pig was greased from head to tail and ears to feet. The contestants would stand in the west end of a freshly watered, muddy arena, until the pig was released in the east end. When the pig started running, the contestants could charge. The winner was anyone who could hold onto the pig until a judge tapped his shoulder. How he held onto the pig was completely up to him.

"Sounds like fun," Henry said.

"I'm with you," I said. "Come on Chance, what do you say?"

"I don't know," said Second Chance. "I hear them pigs can get pretty mean."

As soon as the words left his mouth, he noticed the girls lookin' at him.

"I mean, they get pretty worked up and excited and all. I'd hate to end up hurtin' the little guy tryin' to pin him down."

He knew no one was buyin' it, but he couldn't lose face in front of the girls.

"Oh well, I reckon I'll just be as gentle with him as I can be. Let's do this thing."

I could still see the doubt in Second Chance's eyes and probably should have found an out for him. But then I remembered he had a thumpin' comin'. At least, it would be a fun thumpin'.

We all climbed over the three-foot-tall board fence that enclosed the muddy, makeshift arena. It was an area about fifty feet square and had a good six inches of wall-to-wall mud in it. Several places even had large puddles of standing water.

I looked around at all the contestants sloppin' around in the mud. Nearest to me was Henry, then Second Chance, and a couple more friends of mine from school. Next, were six or seven boys of various ages from the other two schools in the Cove. Then, at the far end of the line, I saw Tyrone Beckett and his cohorts, Kenny, and Jack. Tyrone was staring straight back at me . . . smilin'. I gave a soft groan, thinking; *this may not be the best idea after all.*

The pig was released.

That part about waitin' 'til the pig started runnin' wasn't called for. It was on the move before the judge could get it out of the sack.

We all charged.

You ain't never seen the likes. There were boys slippin', slidin', pushin', shovin', and tryin' to run across the arena, only to go crashin' down in great waves of muddy water. No sooner than they'd go down, they'd be grabbin' the kid closest to them tryin' to get up, only to drag him down too.

It was a crowd-pleasin', mud-flingin' free-for-all, and everybody loved it. A few of us even made it to the far end of the arena—wet and muddy, but still on our feet.

The pig had no idea what all the commotion was about, but he wanted no part of it. He dodged and darted, and frantically searched for any escape he could find. It was easy to tell by the look in his beady eyes that all he wanted to do was to get away from this mob of crazy, mud-covered, Cove boys headed his way.

First one, and then another boy would lunge out and try to grab him, but the frightened, twisting pig simply slipped through their mud-slick hands.

When I saw my chance, I dove for his feet and must have slid a good six feet through the cold muck. All I got for my efforts was a handful of mud and a face full of filth. That, and about ten pounds of wet Cove soil packed into my shirt and pants.

As I started to rise, another contestant landed on top of me, driving me back into the mire. It was a rather harsh blow and I momentarily lost my breath. Not realizing I was in the middle of a large puddle, I gasp in what seemed like a gallon of muddy water before I raised my head enough to breathe. After coughing and spitting out the filth and gasping my lungs full of semi-fresh air, I tried to rise a second time.

"If you know what's good for you, you'll stay down," I heard, as a burst of warm breath blow across my ear. It was Tyrone. I should have known.

He stood up by pushing off the back of my head, driving my face into the mud once more and then slipped and slid toward the fleeing pig.

Second Chance, in all honesty, was just tryin' to stay away from the action. He'd run one way, only to have the pig head that way too. He'd then turn and run another direction and the pig would do the same. Finally, out of pure fear and desperation he tried to climb out of the arena, only to slip on the slick wood fence and tear the inner seam of his pant leg while falling back in. Landing face first and bottom up in the muck, he quickly turned over, jumped up, and continued to flee.

Chance actually thought the muddy beast was chasing him, when of course, in reality, he and the pig were both just tryin' to get to a safe part of the arena where the other one wasn't. They were escaping in the same direction, and a collision was inevitable. And when it happened, it was a doozy.

Second Chance and the pig—both lookin' back over their shoulders at the same time—came crashing together in a massive wall of filth and muddy water. The concussion sent a wave of muck flyin' up the already splattered timber wall and completely drenched several of the screaming, cheering, spectators. While a few women jumped back to avoid the brunt of the slop, most of the enthused crowd didn't even seem to notice the dousing they had just taken.

The more the mud flew in every direction, the more the crowd cheered on Second Chance as he wrestled with the pig.

What the crowd didn't realize amidst all commotion, and couldn't see in the flinging muck and mud, was that one of the pig's rear legs had somehow wound up entangled in the tear in Second Chance's pant leg. The pig was franticly trying to run one way and Second Chance was just as fervently trying to head the other. The pig was squealin' and thrashin', and Chance was screamin' and graspin' his pants, desperately tryin' not to lose his drawers in front of the entire community. To the spectators it appeared that Second Chance had a death grip on the pig with both his hands, and his legs, and they just couldn't get enough of it.

As the battle continued, and the crowd cheered on their gallant hero, a judge came running up. He paused for just a moment, then dodging around trying not to be drawn down into the melee, he slappin' Second Chance on the shoulder signifying a win.

Just then, Chance's pant leg gave way with a final tear releasing the thoroughly frightened pig, and my muddy, bloody, and totally confused friend stood bewildered before a massive crowd of cheering, applauding fans. Even the other contestants who had gathered in a large semi-circle to watch the battle, stood in thigh-high mud, and wildly cheered.

To his absolute astonishment. Second Chance had become champion-greased-pig-catcher of the year.

FOUR

Fireworks

PASTOR STEADMAN OF THE METHODIST Church, one of the four head judges, stood before the crowd. He raised his hands to be recognized, and with a big smile on his face he gave a nod, here and there, and waved to several of his flock.

"I can't remember ever seeing a more exciting, greased pig competition," he said.

A loud cheer echoed across the clearing. Looking around he saw Chance and Abby Fieldman in the crowd.

Pointing at the couple, he said, "Your boy done you proud, Chance."

The crowd gave another cheer and several of the men slapped Chance, Sr., on the back as he smiled from ear to ear and waved. Abby just stood there with a timid grin on her face and tried to make herself small, not being used to, or comfortable with, all the recognition.

"Now bring the champion up here," said Steadman.

Second Chance was pushed and prodded forward lookin' like he was still in the dark about what was goin' on. As he looked around, trying to make sense of all the fuss and bother, he happened to lay eyes on me and Henry. Bein' the true friends that we were, we both immediately began makin' googly eyes and rutting pig faces. Even though Mary hit me in the ribs when she saw what I was doing, I think it helped 'cause it broke the tension for Second Chance and made him snicker.

"That was quite a show, young man," said Pastor Steadman. "Quite a show. And now, for your prize you can choose the very pig that you conquered in battle," Second Chance's eyes 'bout popped out of his head, "or take home one that's already roasted."

Chance, Sr., was about to shout, "Take the live one," when Second Chance blurted out, "I'll take the roasted one."

A cheer rose from the crowd, and Chance, Sr., shrugged, wondering what his boy was thinking.

"You'd think the boy would opt for a pet," he whispered to his wife, rather dumbfounded.

Abby just smiled and taking her husband's right hand in both of hers, leaned her head against his shoulder. She was often saddened and amazed by the thought that a man as good and kindhearted as Chance, Sr., was, could know so very little about his own son.

"Let him enjoy his victory in his own way," she said. "Perhaps he feels he's providing for his family."

At that, Chance, Sr., stood a bit taller. *His boy was becoming a man.*

"You can pick it up right after the fireworks display," Pastor Steadman loudly advised Second Chance as he vigorously shook his hand.

Then turning to the crowd, he said, "Now why don't all you pig chasers go jump into Abrams Creek and give some of that topsoil back to the Cove."

With a cheer, we all charged down to the creek and jumped in fully clothed.

The clear cold water soon turned murky as we splashed around pulling clots of sodden soil off our muddy shirts and trousers and flinging the clumps at each other. It was great fun and in no time at all, we managed to wash off the biggest part of the filth.

As a large stain of darkened water floated around a bend well downstream of us, and the penetrating cold began to settle into our bodies; we started heading toward the shore. With much jostling and laughter, we all climbed the rocky bank and soon flopped down in the thick, tall grass that waited beyond.

I remember looking back at that stream and marveling at how quickly it had returned to its normal state of crystal clarity.

When we were finished "bathing," the church ladies handed out towels so we could dry our hair, faces, and arms. Being a hot summer day, we just let our clothes sun dry on our backs.

In no time at all the glaring July sun began warming our chilled, but refreshed and somewhat cleaner bodies, so me, Henry, and Second Chance got up and headed back toward the picnic grounds.

"That was some mighty fine pig catchin'," Henry teased as we climbed a small embankment where the girls sat waitin' on us. "Hope ya didn't hurt it too bad."

"Yeah and I was hopin' you'd wrangle Pa's hog back into our wagon this evening," I said. "You know, show me, Henry, and Diver how it's done. But now, Pa wouldn't take kindly to you hurting her none."

Second Chance had a distressed and confused look on his face. The last thing he wanted to do was face a full-grown hog.

"Oh, leave him alone," Susan Beckett said, as we neared the girls. "I think he was mighty brave the way he caught that twisting, squealing, muddy pig. And where was you two? You were both just standin' there knee deep in slop with your jaws hangin' open while Chance charged in and conquered the beast all by his lonesome."

Me and Henry pulled up short, kinda hang-dogged and all, not knowing what to say about that. I noticed Mary cover her mouth with her hand and look the other way tryin' unsuccessfully to hide a smile.

"Ah, we was just funnin' him," said Henry.

Susan gave Henry a look that made it clear; the funnin' and the conversation was over. It was kinda funny seein' Henry squirm under the gaze of little Susan Beckett. He didn't seem to know what hit him.

"You want to sit by me, C.J.?" she asked Second Chance.

He nodded and sat down on the embankment near Susan. She scooted over just a tad closer to him and he quickly glanced at me. In his face I saw pride, fear, enchantment, and confusion; all at the same time. He'd been challenged, praised, teased, cheered, frightened, and protected in such a rapid fashion that I don't reckon he had any idea what to think. But I do know without a doubt, that was one day he wasn't ever gonna forget.

It wasn't long before somebody began ringin' a large triangle dinner bell signifyin' the feast was ready. Yes sir, that was what we were all waitin' on and there wasn't a man or beast that was safe if he stood between us and the dinner line. We snatched up plates, stacked 'em high with the finest food the Cove had to offer and found an unoccupied log off by itself to sit on and enjoy our meal.

Me, Henry, and Chance left the girls to protect our food as we hurried over to the Sassafras booth and got some drinks. On the way back, while carrying my drink in one hand and Mary's in the other, I happened to noticed Tyrone and Kenny sneakin' up behind the girls. I couldn't run without spilling the drinks, so I started to shout out a warning.

Just then, Diver came walkin' up and stopped to say something to Mary and Susan. The way he stood there, looking over the girls' heads, I think he was lookin' directly at the bullies. They must have thought so too, because they suddenly turned and went on their way without the girls even knowin' they were being stalked.

Good ol' Diver always seemed to show up when you needed him most.

Later that evening, as the sun was about to set, an announcement was made to gather 'round Orwell's stock pond. The fireworks display was nearly ready. Someone Had drug a mess of logs and stumps over and placed them in a level mowed area along the south edge of the five-acre pond. The fireworks would be fired on the north bank, and with the reflection in the water, the show would be seen from above and below.

Us kids, not wanting to sit with the adults, found a good place along the west shore where the bank had given way. After stomping down the grass, we sat with our feet dangling above the water and had a perfect view of the upcoming events. I sat on one end of our group with Mary next to me. Susan sat on the other side of Mary and patted the ground next to her for Second Chance to sit there. Henry sat on the far end, on the other side of Second Chance. Normally, me and Henry would have sat together, but this time I was glad he took the initiative to let me and Mary be.

The sky darkened and the display began. In years past the bursts had all been primarily orange, but this year, as promised, Orwell had added the new red, white and blue rockets. It was magnificent. Suddenly the old displays that had so thrilled me as a child, seemed drab and boring in comparison. Nothing could top this . . . and then it did.

Three massive bursts of color rent the night sky and sent a crashing boom across the valley that could surely be heard all the way to Knoxville. It was a terrifying and yet exhilarating display. Several cries of surprise were heard among the spectators and Mary suddenly grabbed my hand and hid her face in my shoulder. I don't know if that burst was planned, or if it was a mishap, but at that moment I'd have given Orwell Beckett a year's worth of free labor to do it again.

Throughout the rest of the display, Mary and I held hands and enjoyed the evening. The way my heart was fluttering, in all truth I can say the fireworks took second place. But as they say, all good things must come to an end. The show ended with a fantastic, sky splitting finale. Then everyone, having had a wonderful time, congratulated Orwell, said goodbye to dear friends, and headed for home.

Me and Henry walked Mary to her Pa's coach and helped her climb aboard. The Pastor asked if we'd had a good time and we told him we surely had.

"Good," he said. "Glad to hear it. See you in church on Sunday, Billy. And good seeing you too,

Henry. I had a nice talk with your Ma earlier. She's mighty proud of you. And from what I hear, she has every right to be."

"Thank you, sir," said Henry.

With that, Pastor Wilson nodded and flicked his reins to start their short drive home. Mary looked back and gave me a little wave before her Pa placed a light shawl on her shoulders, which turned her to face the front.

A strange hollowness seemed to settle in my chest, and then Henry slugged me one on the shoulder.

"Billy's got a sweetheart," he teased.

"Aw, shut up," I said hittin' him back.

As we turned to head over to Pa's wagon, I couldn't help but take one more glance back at the Wilson's coach as it faded into the night.

Forrest was loading up his family to drop them off at home while Pa and Diver loaded Pa's hog onto our wagon. They were laughing about the finest third place pig they'd ever seen.

Meanwhile, Miss Melloncamp came riding up in a one-person cart pulled by a pretty, long-haired Shetland pony.

To tell you the truth, I felt kinda sorry for that little pony, seein's how Miss Melloncamp had to have been a good two-hundred-fifty-pounds or better.

"My, what a fine-looking rig," Ma said.

"Why thank you," said Miss Melloncamp. "Orwell Beckett said it was a shame the schoolteacher had to depend on other folks to get around, so he donated this cart and pony to the school."

"Well that was mighty nice of him," said Ma. "Now that you can get around, we'll hafta have you by for dinner some time."

"I'd love to," said Miss Melloncamp. "I happen to be free on Saturday."

"Well I . . ." Ma didn't quite know what to say.

Sarah May, who had been casually listenin' to the conversation as Forrest was preparing to get underway, had to turn her head and cover her mouth to keep from giggling in the rudest of manners.

Ma saw her out of the corner of her eye and had to suppress a grin herself. Sarah always did have a way of tickling Ma with her nonchalant actions.

"Saturday would be just fine," Ma said to Miss Melloncamp. "We'll see you then."

"How lovely," said Miss Melloncamp. "Toodaloo!" she said and pulled away.

"A lot of help you are," Ma called to Sarah May.

"Oh, but Saturday would be just fine," Sarah giggled imitating Ma. Then she turned to Forrest. "You can take me home now," she said.

"Toodaloo!" she called to Ma, and waved with a big grin on her face.

Ma couldn't help but laugh.

When Forrest got back from dropping his family off, we all loaded up into the two conveyances and started our much longer trek across the valley and into the Smoky Mountain foothills. A light mist was settling over the Cove, and I believe I nodded off a time or two before we made it home.

FIVE

Storyteller

IT WAS NEARLY MIDNIGHT before we climbed above the soft mist slowly rising from the valley floor. We passed through the last tendrils of ghostly vapor as it drifted on a light breeze among the darkened veil of obscured underbrush and slowly twisted its way through the reaching arms of shagbark hickories and time hardened oak trees. Above us arched a velvet expanse of coal black skies awash with tens of thousands of stars, exhibiting the glistening glow of the Milky Way.

Upon reaching the cabin, Forrest gave Ma a hug and a kiss on the cheek and told Long Star how much he enjoyed her company at the festivities. Then Pa helped Ma and Long Star down from the carriage, and Forrest began his long drive home.

Ma, Pa, and Long Star entered the cabin. Ma put on some coffee as Long Star placed a couple of pies on the table that she brought back from the celebration. The women knew that when we got home everyone would be in the mood for a late-night snack. As for all the men folk; anytime was the right time for a late-night snack.

Hurrying as fast as they could, Henry helped Diver return the grumpy hog to his pen. He hadn't been impressed by the journey or the celebration and he didn't take kindly to his usual routine being so rudely interrupted.

While they wrestled with the hog, I started the overdue milking of the also frustrated cow and goat. You know, some things in nature just ain't designed for waitin' and an overfull utter is one of 'em.

"I'm sure sorry 'bout this," I told Tilly as I poured grain into her feed trough. As I talked to her I reached over and smoothed a scuffed-up section of short orange-brown hair on her side.

"I know you're mighty uncomfortable and it's all my fault, but I'll have you feelin' better in no time."

As I settled down on my milkin' stool and was busy positioning the oaken milk bucket, she swished her tail coating my sleeve with a bit of the days muck. I'm not saying it was on purpose, but she did look back as if to see if she got me. I'm guessin' my apology was not accepted.

When the hog was settled and appeased with a special treat for bringing Pa such good fortune, Diver and Henry came and helped me finish up. Then Diver told us to go ahead. He had something else to take care of and then he'd be right along. We didn't need tellin' twice. We rushed the fresh milk over to the springhouse, grabbed a cold jug o' milk and headed for the cabin.

"Where's Diver?" asked Pa, as we plopped down at the table.

"He said he had somethin' he needed to take care of and then he'd be right along," I said.

"Okay," said Pa, with a knowing look in his eye. "Well then I reckon we'll just wait on him. Go get my checker set."

I hopped up and retrieved Pa's checkers from the trunk where he kept 'em. I knew Henry and Long Star had never played the game and Pa would have a jolly ol' time teachin' it to 'em. But I also wished Diver would hurry up. Even after competing in the pie eatin' contest earlier, I don't reckon I'd had my fill 'cause my mouth was waterin' just thinkin' about them two pies sittin' on the table.

Pa sat across from Long Star and Henry with the checkerboard laid out on the table and placed all the chips in their starting positions.

"This is a game of strategy," he said. "Don't feel bad if it takes a bit to catch on. Nothin' worthwhile in life is easy right off. Just hang in there and you'll get it."

The first game was to teach them the rules. Long Star had trouble with planning ahead for future moves and kept settin' herself up to lose multiple pieces. Pa showed her where her mistakes were bein' made, but she didn't seem to be catching on.

That wasn't the case with Henry. By his second game with Pa, I think I saw a light begin to glow in Henry's eyes and about halfway through, it seemed Pa was beginning to struggle a bit. (Henry always was uncommonly quick at catchin' on to new things.) It was gettin' interesting, but I can't really say who would have won 'cause Diver showed up and the game was put to the side. Fact is, it didn't seem Pa was all that upset about the interruption.

"I think you're getting it," he said to Henry. "Some time we'll hafta play a real game. Now let's see what Diver's been up to."

The look in Pa's eyes told me he knew exactly what Diver had been up to. And as I glanced around, I noticed Ma standin' there with her hands clutched before her chest, slowly wringing her apron, and lightly chewing on her lower lip.

She never did have much of a poker face.

Long Star on the other hand was a bit harder to read, but I believe I saw a twinkle in her eye as well.

"Got something here for you boys," Diver said, as he crossed the kitchen floor and stood before me and Henry. He pulled his hands out from behind his back and dangled a necklace in front of each of us.

Me and Henry glanced at each other and then in unison reached up and took the proffered gifts. They were magnificent. I laid mine in the palm of my hand and leaning a bit closer to the lantern sitting in the center of the table, tried to get a better look. As I ran my finger across the exquisite object, I marveled at the wonderful workmanship.

It was a leather cord rubbed smooth with bee's wax and crimped with small gold bands equally spaced every two inches around its length. A long panther claw set in a beautiful gold fitting hung from the center. The fitting featured a delicate carving of our initials placed within the outline of a mountain and underscored with what appeared to be a single bone. I figured Diver must have made a mistake when he handed them to us 'cause mine had an HR on it and Henry's had a BB.

On each side of the fitting, separated by two thin gold disks, there were three, small, polished stones. The first stone on each side was a perfect bead of orangish-tan dolomite smoothed to a high sheen and hand drilled to accommodate the cord. Next, after a pair of gold disks, came a set of two-inch long tubes of black cave onyx infused with brilliant white swirls. It was obvious that the glistening tubes had required many long, patient hours of hand polishing to reach such a perfect form. Then, after another set of gold disks came a final pair of stones. These were once again highly polished beads similar to the first set in shape and size but this time made of nearly translucent red agates of the purest hue. I had never seen such beautiful colors and craftsmanship.

"Those are called storyteller necklaces," said Diver. "They are to help remind you of your youthful adventures many years from now when age will try to make the memories fade.

"The cord is made of leather, which represents the tough existence of life in the mountains. But the leather is coated with bee's wax to smooth the rough surface and bring out the beauty of the material, just as the Creator soothes a receptive mind and reveals the bountiful beauty all around us.

"The gold bands spaced along the cord represent friends and family who travel through every chapter of your journey with you. They come and go in their proper time and way, but each shines like the golden luster of the purest of all earthly materials.

"The panther's claw hanging from the fitting at the center of the necklace representing the ultimate cause of your great adventure. The dolomite stones on each side of the fitting were collected from the sleeping chamber where your adventure began. The black and white swirls of the cave onyx which came from the gravel bed were you laid in darkness and despair, represent your journey back into the morning light and renewed hope. The red agates are from the pool below the falls and represent returning to your families after escaping the clutches of the mountain.

"The two gold disks between the stones represent the two days of darkness you spent without seeing the golden rays of the sun, having only each other to rely on.

"And finally, the fitting. The fitting is made of gold and holds the entire necklace together just as your friendship and faith in each other enabled you to pull together and survive all the terrors that came your way.

"The HR on yours, Billy, and the BB on Henry's, inscribed in the mountain, are a reminder of the friendship that got you through this ordeal.

"It also has a single bone below the initials representing the discovery of the legendary Moss Zeekman. Three people shared that cold, gravel ledge; but a single bone means two survived.

"As for the gold used to make the fittings, disks and bands; it came from two of Moss Zeekman's coins. Those coins will be with you boys for the rest of your lives."

Henry and I both sat stunned. Neither of us had ever imagined receiving such a gift.

"When, and how?" I said.

"Well, it was a collaboration between all four of us," Diver said, indicating himself, Ma, Pa, and Long Star.

"Your Pa and I went back to the canyon falls to give Moss Zeekman's bones a proper burial. While we was there, we retrieved Tudwell's rope and I found the two gold coins, and the black cave onyx where you boys slept.

"After burying Moss, I searched through the gravel at the pool below the falls and found the agate stones.

"Later, when we talked to Long Star about making a memento of your quest, she mentioned the Indian storytelling necklace. It was perfect.

"After that I returned to the sleeping chamber and found the dolomite, and with some leather cordage from your Pa's tanning shed, we had all the materials we needed.

"Your Pa made all the molds for the gold fittings, disks, and bands, from ball lead. He used his ammo forge to melt and pour the gold. He also worked the leather and smoothed it with bee's wax. I shaped and drilled out the stones and etched the fittings, and Kate and Long Star spent days polishing the stones and gold to bring out the high-quality luster you see. Then I just had to put it all together."

Me and Henry sat teary eyed admiring the wonderful gifts and contemplating all the work put into them.

"I don't know what to say," I said. "Thank you."

Henry simply nodded his head and said, "Me too," and hugged his Ma.

Everybody was smiling. Then Ma suddenly rushed over and gave me and Henry both long hugs and an embarrassing kiss on the cheek; what with Pa and Diver lookin' on.

Then Pa said, "Billy, there's one more thing for you."

Henry smiled and stood back to watch what would happen next.

"We already talked this over with Henry, and he agreed that because you insisted that he take the larger portion of the gold, you should get this," said Pa.

With that, Diver stepped outside and soon returned with a bundle in his arms. Pa removed the lantern from the table, and my knees went weak when Diver rolled it out. It was the panther's hide. Nearly eight feet of beautiful, tawny, mountain lion carefully tanned for a life-sized rug. I was flabbergasted. I looked around at everyone, and then settled on Pa.

"Thank you," I said. "I'll treasure it always."

Pa nodded and smiled, then rather awkwardly pulled me to him and gave me a hug. Then, clearing his throat and letting me go, he said, "I think I heard somebody say something about a pie."

We all laughed and quickly cleared the table.

I'm sure that pie was wonderful, 'cause I ain't ever ate one that wasn't, but in all honesty, I can't say

I remember it. My mind was too busy swirlin' with thoughts of the storyteller necklace and panther rug.

If you'd've seen me 'bout then, I think I may've been floating about twelve inches above my chair. And I didn't come down until long after Long Star took my sleeping loft and me and Henry went out to the barn to sleep at Diver's place.

Diver climbed up to his room, but me and Henry decided to stay in the tool area below. I rolled out my sleeping mat and Henry shook the dust from an old saddle blanket and spread it out on the floor. Of course, we were both too worked up to sleep, so we just sat there bathed in the glow of a big tallow candle and admired our new necklaces.

"Ain't this somethin'?" said Henry.

"It surely is." I agreed.

And with that we gently rubbed each stone, disk, band, and the big claw in the necklaces as we recited and relived our great adventure. They truly were story telling necklaces and I knew in my heart we would neither ever forget.

SIX

Dream

SUNUP FOUND TWO HAND standing straight and silent in the front yard. I saw him from a small window in the tool storage area of the barn when I happened to glance out as I was rollin' up my sleeping mat. No matter how many times I witnessed that old man's sudden arrival, I was still mystified by the shaman. He always seemed to just appear. It was never a matter of lookin' off in the distance and sayin', "Hey, there's old Two Hand comin' this way." No, he was simply there, or he wasn't.

As I watched, I noticed a steady column of white smoke curled from the chimney top of our cabin before drifting away on a gentle morning breeze. Ma was up and fixin' to begin breakfast.

Pa soon came out with two large mugs o' coffee in his hands and greeted Two Hand by handing him a steaming cup. The old man smiled and sipped the dark brew without bothering to let it cool. If he got scalded, he didn't let on, he simply nodded his approval, and took a second sip.

As they strolled across the yard and sat on some stumps Pa had placed below an old hickory tree, I turned away and gave a still sleepin' Henry a nudge on the leg with my foot. I then crossed the breezeway into the front barn where I was greeted by an impatiently waiting cow and goat. With full udders and hankerin' for a big scoop of grain while being milked, they weren't figurin' on no tardiness like they'd witnessed the night before.

Another day on the homestead had begun.

With the chores done and a quick trip out back accomplished, me and Henry grabbed a bar of lye soap and got cleaned up down at the creek before snatchin' a jug o' milk from the springhouse and charging in to see what Ma had on for breakfast.

When we arrived, Long Star had just finished settin' the meal. Ham, bread, fresh butter, blackberry jam, sliced tomatoes from Ma's garden, and coffee, and milk, adorned the old, oak-plank table. Ma had just filled two plates each with six fried eggs and all the fixings and asked me to take them out to Pa and Two Hand. She then told Henry, he might oughta take the coffee pot and refill their mugs too.

By the time we returned Diver had come in, and after a quick blessing, Ma set a large platter of fried eggs on the table, and we commenced to making it disappear. And I'll tell ya true, them eggs didn't stand a chance.

After breakfast we all gathered in the front yard to say our goodbyes and to wish Long Star, Two Hand, and Henry a safe trip home. All that is except for Diver, who headed for the barn. Pa told Two Hand he had somethin' for him and stepped into the house only to return moments later with one of his prize Bowie knives in a fine tooled sheath.

"For you, my friend," he said, handing the knife to Two Hand.

Two Hand slowly pulled the knife from its sheath and admired the high sheen blade. He tested the weight, the balance, and the razor-sharp edge of the long fighting weapon. His hand caressed the polished walnut handle, the s curved brass guard, and the two-inch sharpened upper clip, equally useful for back-slashing in a fight, or skinning prey. The thing was a marvel in modern technology and far superior to anything Two Hand had ever owned before.

64

"It is a fine blade," said Two Hand. "A gift of honor; of brotherhood. I have nothing to compare to give you in return."

"I remember the young boy you pulled from the grasp of death," Pa said. "Who, many years later, you befriended, watched over, and taught the ways of the mountains. Who, you encouraged to become his own man, despite his flaws, and with an honest view of his accomplishments? It was you who risked your own life to save that of a child you didn't even know. It is I who have no gift to compare."

"I thank you, Zebulon," he said, strapping the sheath onto his soft, deer-skin belt. "I shall honor the giver each time I use it."

As we stood around watchin' the exchange, no one had noticed Diver recross the bridge and walk up behind us with the goat on a short cord leash.

"Well, I hope I'm not imposing on this little get together," he said as we all turned to see him standing there.

Then Diver spoke to Long star, "Me, Kate, and Zeb have noticed how you take a mighty fancy to goat's milk when you're here. And seein's how we got more milk than we can use from the ol' Tilly, we figured you might could take this old ornery nanny off our hands."

He held out the lead cord to Long Star.

She just stood there staring at the goat for a bit before lookin' at Diver, and then at Pa, and finally settling on Ma. "I don't know what to say," she said.

"Just say yes," said Ma. "We really don't need her, and you would be doin' us a favor by takin' her off our hands."

"Yeah," I said. "Henry already knows how to milk her. And I don't figure he has enough chores to do anyway."

Everyone laughed except Henry, who grimaced. He knew I was more than pleased to have one less chore of my own.

"I don't know how to thank you," said Long Star, admiring her new goat.

"Don't mention it," said Pa. "Enjoy. Besides, I been thinkin' 'bout gettin' some ducks for Billy to milk."

That brought a round of laughs and giggles. I half-heartedly joined in, not a hundred percent sure Pa was joking. You can't really milk a duck can you?

After Two Hand and the Rainwaters left, Pa turned to Ma and said, "Looks like everybody got somethin' but you Ma."

She took his arm with both her hands and looked up into his face. "I got everything I need," she said.

He grinned. "That may be," he said, "but you ain't got left out. You're just gonna hafta wait. It's a-comin'."

"What's a-comin'," Ma asked? She stepped back with her hands on her hips claspin' her dish towel in one fist as she looked up and strained to see Pa's grinning face darkened by the clear blue sky behind him.

"Ha," he laughed. "You're just gonna hafta wait. I reckon it won't be more than a week or two."

"You're a cruel man, Zebulon Banion." Ma said, as she hit him across the chest with her dish cloth in a mock display of anger.

"And you're a sweetheart," he said. "A mighty inquisitive sweetheart."

Ma shook her head and gave up, knowin' she wouldn't get a thing out of Pa 'til he was willin' to give it. She dramatically huffed off to the house to do her breakfast cleanup.

Pa watched her go and chuckled to himself. This next week or so was gonna be mighty tough on her, but she'd get over it when she saw what he got her.

About that time, Diver came walking up and said, "Zeb, I've been thinkin'."

"Well, that ain't such a bad thing to do," said Pa. "I been accused of doin' it a time or two myself. Not to say I'm on your level of thinkin', but I do try."

Diver grinned and snorted. "You're in a good mood this mornin'," he said.

"Yep, it's a fine mornin'," said Pa.

"Well, what I've been thinkin' is, the corn is fixin' to tassel right quick now. It might not be a bad idea to be collectin' that honey I told you about and movin' that hive on over near the cornfield."

Pa lifted his hat and scratched an itchy spot on top his head. "I reckon you're right there," he said. "Guess we better figure out how we're gonna house that colony once we catch 'em."

"Done got it figured," said Diver. "There's a big old hollow black gum tree on that knoll just east of the field. Way I see it, we hang the brood comb in there and box in the queen for a day or two, and those bees will take right to it."

"Sounds good to me," said Pa. "How much honey you reckon we'll get outta the old hive?"

"Hard to say," said Diver, "but from the action I saw around it, it ain't gonna be no minor haul."

"Okay," said Pa, "we'll take a five-gallon barrel and a few buckets. That should 'bout cover it, I reckon."

With that, they got busy loadin' the wagon and hitchin' up the team. I pondered on asking to go along, but then had second thoughts about it. I never did have me too much of a hankerin' to be stung. That rock throwin' incident I had with them wasps that Pa liked to laugh about made a believer outta me. I decided I could probably find a less painful way to spend the day. But it turned out, Ma found it for me.

'Billy," she called, "come fetch me a bucket o' water."

"Sure Ma," I called back.

Headed to the house to get the freshwater bucket, I looked back and waved to Diver, as he and Pa rode away. It come over me then, that I just might've made a mistake. If it come to dodgin' bees or doin' chores, I reckon the bees might not've been that bad. Oh well, nothin' for it now.

Pa had left Ma's freshwater bucket, so I ran into the kitchen and grabbed it. Then I rushed down to the creek, and being careful not to snatch any moss or catch a crawdad or nothin'; Ma didn't take kindly to that at all, I drew it 'bout three-quarters-full and toted it back to the house.

"Thank you, Billy," Ma said. "Now take these breakfast scraps and mix 'em in some of our leftover goat's milk and slop the pigs."

"Yes, Ma," I said.

"And when you're done with that, I need you to go to the springhouse and scrape the cream off all the fresh milk and churn it for butter. Take this here jug with ya to pour off the buttermilk. We're about out. Be sure to do the churning in the springhouse where it's cool or you won't ever get it separated in this heat. And don't salt the butter. I'll do that this evening when I mold it."

Yep, I was thinking, I done made a mistake by not going with Pa and Diver. Ma always got herself all worked up 'bout doing chores and what-not when she got all anxious; like waitin' to see what Pa had got her, and if ya happened to be the nearest one to her, it just naturally spilled right over on you.

Oh well, sloppin' pigs and fillin' their water trough weren't no big deal, and while churnin' butter took a bit a work, at least I'd be sittin' in the springhouse rather than in the hot sun. And truth be told, it wouldn't take but an hour or so anyway.

"Okay Ma," I said, snatchin' up the bowl of leftovers and rushing out before she could think of anything else for me to do.

You know, by the time I was done; having been up half the night before with Henry, I was plumb tired. And coming out of that cool, shaded springhouse into the hot sun didn't help a bit. I kinda slunk around watchin' out for Ma and tryin' to avoid any more chores. I finally snuck over to the barn where me and Henry had slept. My panther hide was still rolled up over there and tied with a leather cord.

That little window in the tool storage area always seemed to have a nice cool breeze off the creek blowing through it. I kinda figured on a hot summer day like that the work bench in front of that window would make a mighty refreshin' place to take a nap.

Leaving my reed mat rolled up, I spread out my panther hide rug on the bench and laid down on it to try it out . . . Wonderful! The hide was amazingly soft, and I think Ma must have rubbed a little lavender into it 'cause it smelled fantastic.

A cool breeze caressed my hot skin as I laid there in front of the window. I even felt a tiny ripple-like shiver as a bead of sweat trickled down my back.

It didn't take long before my mind gently drifted away, leaving the barn and its varied scents of leather tack, stored hay, and dried mule droppings, far behind.

I was adrift on a flowing river of midnight black. Darkness engulfed me on every side. It was as if the world had faded away and left me floating in a sea of endless space—infinite nothingness.

As I drifted, I realized all sensations of touch, sight, sound and smell had also abandoned me. It was as if my mind was the only thing in the realm of reality. The only thing in existence.

I tried to lift my hand before my eyes. Nothing. There are no hands in nothingness. No legs, no arms, no eyes. I should have been in a state of terror but oddly enough, I was at peace. I guess when all else fades, fear goes with it.

Then I saw a spark—a distant light. The glistening gleam of a remote star. No, not a single star, but a thousand stars, far . . . far away. The softest of glows—yet piercing in the velvety display before me.

I reached for that light with my nothing arms and drew it near. A flickering flame dripped tallow on my exposed hand. A hand that felt the hot sting from a candle burned to the stump, clinging to life as its wick dipped below the lavender scented wax.

And in the flickering light of the candle's faltering glow a face appeared. It was the face of a massive beast whose snarling muzzle blocked the night sky; whose hot and putrid breath flowed around great stalactite-like fangs as they crashed down on cracked and bleeding stalagmite canines below.

A mighty hiss escaped the cavernous throat as scythe-like claws flashed golden streaks through the dark chamber restricting my every move. I thrust my arms before my face and felt a warm rush of liquid night wash across my limbs and sweep me with an irresistible flow into a hollow nothingness with a heart-stopping plunge, as if over a towering waterfall. Twisting and turning, I silently screamed as I plummeted into a bottomless abyss.

I awoke when my sweat-soaked body crashed onto the rough-sawn, hardwood floor beneath the work bench.

But my struggle continued as I strove to escape from the twisted folds of the panther's hide which seemed to be grasping me.

Once free, I scooted backward on hands and heels across the room, finally coming to rest against a large support post. Trembling, I gasped for breath and stared at the crumpled, mountain lion rug lying on the floor.

You may call me yellow if you will, but I decided right then and there it would be a long, long, time before I ever slept on that hide again.

Pa and Diver came in grinnin' from ear to ear that night, and they thrilled Ma with nearly a hundred pounds of some of the finest honey you ever saw.

As she nursed their numerous bee stings, they had a great time just a jokin' and a laughin'. They were both trying to tell the bigger whopper 'bout how the other went to hoppin' and fetchin' every time a bee put up a bit of defense for its hive.

Seems them bees knew exactly what their God givin' defenses were for, and weren't the least bit scared to use 'em neither.

Anyway, a couple hours of minor pain and they finally managed to clean out the hive and move the queen with her brood comb, and as many workers and drones as they could catch, to Diver's hollow black gum tree over near the cornfield.

Pa said the rest of the colony would find the new hive soon enough and settle in. And about the time they got settled, the corn would tassel out and them bees would be so busy haulin' pollen back to the hive, you wouldn't be able to drive 'em outta there if you wanted to.

What with all the jokin' and whatnot goin' on between Pa and Diver, no one seemed to notice that I was a bit quieter than normal that night. My new necklace and panther rug never came up in conversation and I reckon it would have been a bit of an awkward discussion if it had so I was grateful.

Both gifts were prized possessions and I loved them dearly, but I figured they should probably adorn my wall for a spell.

You know, may as well not take the chance of losin' or damagin' them; if you know what I mean,

SEVEN

Battle of The Schoolmarm

EARLY SATURDAY MORNIN', Pa strained about twenty pounds or so of pure honey through a linen cloth. Three passes and he figured it was 'bout as clean of impurities as he could get it. He then poured it into a freshly fire-singed oak bucket and tied a piece of burlap over the top to keep flies and dust out of it on his trip down to Clarence's place.

"I'll be off now," he called to Ma as he placed the bucket in the back of the wagon.

Ma came out and stood on the front stoop with one hand on her waist and the other shading her eyes from the midmorning sun. "Now don't you be down there beatin' Clarence at checkers all day, Zebulon," she said. "You know Miss Melloncamp is coming for dinner and I want you here."

Pa kinda grumbled something under his breath before saying, "Yes, dear," as he climbed up into the seat of his wagon and released the handbrake. He then snapped the team into motion.

As he rattled across the yard and onto the rutted trail that led to the Cove, I heard him whistling a tune. I believe it was, "That Old Oaken Bucket."

I always did admire Pa's strong, clear whistle and that's what was my downfall that day. Instead of hightailin' it and findin' an out-of-the-way place to spend my time (Ma still hadn't received her gift from Pa), I hesitated to listen to Pa and the next thing I heard was Ma callin'.

"Billy, I need you to fetch me a couple a turnips, along with a mess of greens, and about a pint of buttermilk, a slab of venison, a little pork belly, and a bucket of spring water."

"Yes Ma," I said. Yep, Pa's tune done got me.

I finally got all the fixin's together for Ma and she said she was gonna make pulled venison and dumplin's, along with turnips and greens; one of my favorite meals, so I couldn't complain none. And then she goes and says I need to be headed down to the creek and get scrubbed up.

"Oh, Ma," I said, but she wasn't havin' it. She grabbed a bar of lye soap off a kitchen shelf and threw it to me.

"Here's a brand-new bar I just boiled down the other day," she said. "Next time I see you, I want to see a glow on that face."

Diver had just come in as she said that and couldn't help but chuckle at my long face. "Hang in there, boy," he said. "Even ol' Andy Jackson's got to knock the trail dust off now and then."

He smiled and thought it was a great joke until Ma grabbed another bar and threw it at him.

"And here's one for you too," she said. "Won't hurt you none to spend some time in the creek your own self."

"But Kate," Diver said.

Ma cut him off right there. "Don't you be a 'but Katein' me," she said. "You, Billy, and ol' Andy Jackson ain't none gonna be dirty faced in my kitchen when I got company a comin'. So, if you're fixin' on eatin' this afternoon, I suggest you head on down to the creek and scrub that filth off o' ya."

When you're beat, you're beat. We headed on down to the creek.

When Pa got home, me and Diver were both sittin' at the kitchen table drinkin' cold buttermilk. Pa sat down and looked at the two of us.

"What happened to you two?" he said.

We were both sittin' there with big ol' red, puffy faces and hands, looking like we'd been strapped down in the blarin' sun for the last week or so. We both looked at Ma.

She kinda hung her head a bit and tried to stifle a persistent grin. I'm not real sure if it was due to guilt, embarrassment, or hilarity, but she finally conquered the impulse.

"I reckon it was my fault," she said. "I made both of 'em go take a bath, and it may be that I made that last batch of lye soap a bit too strong."

Pa sat there for a short time and then burst out in laughter. "If you two don't look like a pair of scalded hogs," he said. "Makes me want to go fetch my scrapin' knife and finish the job."

He found it mighty funny. He sat there slappin' the table, carryin' on, and havin' a good old time until Ma kinda puffed up and began gettin' red herself. She then grabbed a bar of soap off the top shelf and threw it at him.

"Here's the last bar of the old batch," she said. "You don't exactly smell like peaches and flowers yourself. Now go get cleaned up. Miss Melloncamp will be here in an hour, or so."

Pa was still chucklin' as he went out the backdoor and headed for the creek.

"I ain't so sure that bar was from the old batch," Diver told Ma.

"Yeah, it is." Ma said, "I kept the old batch on the top shelf."

"You surely did," said Diver. "But remember the other day when you was doin' wash and asked me to get you a bar of soap. I'm sure I grabbed the last one off the top shelf and gave it to ya."

Ma had a quizzical look on her face. "Well then, where did that bar come from?"

Pa was still laughin' as he lathered up two big handfuls of lavender scented lye soap and went to scrubbin' his face. In less than six seconds he knew he'd made a mistake.

"Ye-ow!" he bellowed, as the lye went to work. In no time he was face down, fully clothed, in the cold creek just a splashin' and a scrubbin'. Unlike Diver and me, who had simply rubbed our face and hands with the bar of soap; Pa had planted his face in a huge pile of lather. The more splashin' and rubbin' he did, the more them suds worked their way into his eyes, causin' him to rub even harder.

It was a mighty unpleasant few minutes for all of us. What with Pa in the creek just a bellowin' to beat the band, and the rest of us in the kitchen listenin' to the fray. I can't say I ever knowed a raging-bear-facing-mountain-man could put up such a fuss, but that day I learned he sure could. And there was something else I learned too. Not one of us made a move to help. I reckon some things a man's just gotta face on his own.

When Miss Melloncamp arrived, I took her cart and pony and tied them in the shade under that big yellow butternut tree I used to like to sit in. She was starin' at me mighty strange-like, but I just acted like there was nothing wrong and invited her into the house.

When we entered, I plopped down next to Diver and Ma looked up from where she was ladling out the venison and dumplings.

"Hello, Miss Melloncamp," she said. "I'm so glad you could join us. Please have a seat at the table. Dinner is just about ready. Hope you like venison and dumplings."

"Oh yes," she said, "that sounds marvelous."

She stood there for a moment glancing at the male members of the family, probably wondering what kind of strange ailment only attacks the men. Then Pa looked up at her with his big, blood-red eyes, looking like ol' Slewfoot himself, and said in a rather hoarse voice, "Have a seat, Miss Melloncamp."

She gave a nervous little smile and shuffled her great bulk around the table, staying as far away from Pa as possible, and sat on the very end of the bench with me and Diver.

It was a fine meal and Miss Melloncamp tried her hardest not to let her discomfort interfere with it. She pretty much kept her head down as she ate, hoping to avoid looking at the menfolk. She only glanced up to politely answer a question from Ma now and then. The food was her refuge; but alas, she could only eat two platefuls, along with quite a mess of turnips, greens, and about a half a loaf of bread.

"I must truly apologize," she said to Ma, "but unfortunately, I have pressing business back in the Cove that can't wait. It was a lovely meal, and I do appreciate the invitation."

"Oh, you hafta leave so soon?" said Ma. "What a pity, I'm sure Zeb was looking forward to playing checkers with you."

Miss Melloncamp made the mistake of looking over at Pa with his terrifying red eyes just as he chomped down on a slice of stewed turnip. The red turnip juice gathered at the corner of his mouth and began to run down on his chin before he wiped it off with the back of his hand. She shuddered and said, "Oh, I know it's a shame, but a schoolmarm's work is never done."

With that, she once again complimented Ma on a fine meal as she shuffled herself back around the table, still staying as far away from Pa as possible.

I suppose at that point, you might be thinkin' everything had went as good as possible under the circumstances. Ma was a bit embarrassed by her menfolk and all, but she'd offered up a good meal that certainly hadn't been ignored by her guest, and she'd played the host to the best of her ability. She had fulfilled her duty as a conscientious member of the Cove community, and no one could blame her if her guest happened to have urgent plans preventing her from staying longer.

You know, all in all, you might figure things could have gone worse. And wouldn't you know it? When they can, they usually do.

As Miss Melloncamp started across the yard for her cart, that big ol' woman hating, Leghorn rooster of Ma's saw her coming.

Me, Ma, Diver, and Pa had all gathered at the door stoop, but I reckon I'm the first one who saw what was about to happen, and not knowing what else to do, I shouted out a loud warning.

A quite startled Miss Melloncamp glanced back at the crowd of red-faced menfolk watching her and with a concerned look on her face, she picked up the pace toward her pony cart.

Then as she turned back around, she suddenly found herself face to face with a giant Leghorn rooster just a flapping and a cackling as he flew down from the chicken coop roof.

No more did he touch down then the chase was on. He took in after her full-out and head-on like he was a Spanish fighting bull, and she was dressed in a matador's cape.

She screamed out loud and forgot all about her cart. In an instant, she was headed for the Cove trail with her arms a waving and her bulk a floppin'. Truth is, I was mighty impressed by how quickly she was movin' when she left that yard.

Ma, on the other hand, was in shock.

"Zeb! Zeb! Go, help, her!" she stammered loudly. "Billy, catch that rooster! Diver, get her cart!"

We all jumped to it but knew right off, it wasn't gonna be an easy task. Miss Melloncamp had done made it to the Cove trail and was sidesteppin' the worst of the erosion ruts while keepin' up a pace that would have shown mighty well at Orwell's 4th of July celebration foot races. It didn't appear she was losing a whole lot of ground to that rooster, but I don't reckon she saw it that way. She was just a screamin' and a blubberin' as she went. Her dress was all bellowed out. Her hair was flappin' in the wind. And I saw one shoe go flying out over a hillside where it may never be found.

Believe it or not, losing that shoe helped her out for a bit. Her left foot with the shoe, was landing in a rut, and her bare right foot was striking on top a ridge which kept her level for a good twenty feet or so.

If she could just hold out a bit longer, me and Pa were almost there. I wanted to let her know, so I hollered out, and made a grab for the rooster.

Right then, she glanced back and saw me charging behind her with my arms spread wide, and Pa's big, red eyes close behind me. She screeched anew and picked up her pace a bit.

Though I can't imagine what the Leghorn thought he was going to do with Miss Melloncamp once he caught her, he had just begun to launch himself when I took a flying leap and grabbed his splayed out, sharp-clawed feet. We both went crashing to the ground as he flapped, and clawed, and pecked at my arms, still not wanting to give up the chase.

Pa leaped over me and the Leghorn and began calling Miss Melloncamp to let her know it was okay.

"Miss . . . Miss," he was shouting between breaths. She was having none of it. She kept up the pace.

Finally, he drew close enough to reach out his massive hand and lay it on her shoulder. She screamed once more as she looked back into his bloodshot eyes. Then she spun around and clocked him upside the jaw with her not so massive fist, but with two hundred and fifty pounds of terrified schoolmarm behind it.

Both Pa's feet shot out from under him and I witnessed him make a mighty rough landin' on his backside right there in the middle of the trail.

In the meantime, the momentum spun Miss Melloncamp on around and her single shoeless foot missed its landing on the ridgetop tangling her feet and causing her to wind up on her backside in an enormous washed out rut in the road. Her head was pointed downhill with her outer dress flung up over it and her legs were straight up in the air, still kicking like she had never stopped running.

"Oh, oh, oh," she was crying with both arms flapping, but unable to turn herself over.

It was then that Diver, in Miss Melloncamp's cart, finally caught up with us and took in the scene.

I was doing everything I could to keep that crazy rooster under control. Pa was sittin' in the trail just a rubbin' his jaw. And poor Miss Melloncamp was in a quite undignified situation.

"Well, help her get up," growled Pa.

Diver quickly climbed out of the cart, and with no little effort, helped Miss Melloncamp to her feet. He awkwardly tried to help brush her off, but she pushed him away, sniffled, and climbed aboard her cart. With a quick snap of the reins she trotted on down the trail as fast as that little pony could pull her.

I guess in circumstances like that, goodbyes aren't called for.

It was a ragged, dirty, downtrodden group of menfolk that stood in front of Ma when we made it back up the hill. We were all kinda hang-dogged and apologetic and all, even though I didn't quite see how we were to blame. I mean, we didn't want to bathe in the first place, and it was Ma's rooster that caused the trouble.

But Pa and Diver didn't bring it up, so I didn't either. I just stood there holdin' that crazy rooster who looked at Ma and gave a sweet little chortle like he had no idea what all the hubbub was about.

EIGHT

A Whole New Hearth

THAT NEXT WEEK TURNED out to be rather hectic. On Sunday we went to church as usual and sat in our normal pew. I reckon there was more than a few curious glances thrown our way, what with me, Pa, and Diver looking like we had a world class case of sunburn.

Who'd've ever thought a lye burn could take up to two weeks to heal?

And on top of that, Pa sat there with a swollen cheek, and a downright manly shade of bruising encircling his flaming red left eye—which just couldn't help but give you the willies if you looked at it. I guess it would have even given Jud Beckett himself pause.

Miss Melloncamp, who normally sat two rows in front of us, had for some reason chosen to sit on the other side of the church all the way up front. She was about as far from us as she could get. And it didn't escape my notice that her chosen seat gave her quick access to the back door of the church - just in case she needed it, I suppose.

I was a bit amused that Pastor Wilson had chosen that week to preach on the blessings that the Israelites had waitin' for them in Caanan, a land flowing with milk and honey. Kinda like our own homestead since Diver had come along. But as I mulled over that thought, I suddenly got downright tickled. You know, the Israelites didn't even know how blessed they were that not a single chicken was mentioned!

After church, Forrest and Sarah May stood out front and listened to Pa and Ma tell all about our previous day's exploits. They wanted to hear every detail, and often broke in to have a point clarified before wailing with laughter once again. To tell the truth, I was gettin' a bit concerned about Sarah May. She was laughin' so hard she couldn't've been gettin' enough air. I was afraid she was gonna pass out right there in the churchyard.

With all the gaiety going on, several other people drifted our way to see what was so amusing, but when Pa looked up with those wild-beast eyes of his, they tended to change there minds and went their own ways.

When the tale was finally told to everyone's satisfaction and the tears of laughter were wiped away, Forrest gave Pa a letter he had received just the night before from Delma. Since Walt Carrol, who hauled mail into the Cove every couple of weeks or so, didn't deliver to the outlying homesteads, he left Pa's mail with Forrest.

Concern showed on Pa's face as he quickly opened the missive and scanned the delicate cursive within. It didn't take long for his countenance to soften and he smiled down into the anxious face of Ma.

"She says it's about time," said Pa. "She wants to know if we can come be with her in Maryville."

"Oh, can we, Zeb?" Ma pleaded. She grabbed Pa's arm and looked up into his amazingly less severe looking face.

"Just as soon as we get packed," he said.

Noticing the date at the end of the letter he said, "This must have been one of the last letters Walt picked up. It's dated Thursday, just three days ago."

"Oh, come on, let's hurry Zeb," Ma said as she climbed into the wagon without even waitin' for his help.

Forrest was grinning as he shook Pa's hand. "Give me and Sarah's best wishes to Delma," he said. "And by the way, that package you talked to Orwell about has arrived. By the time you get back it will all be ready."

"I appreciate that son," Pa said.

"Come on Zeb, let's get to movin'," urged Ma.

Pa grinned and slapped Forrest's arm. "I reckon I better get goin' before your ma leaves without me," he said.

Forrest laughed, and gave a small wave, "God's speed," he said.

When we arrived home, Ma went straight to work getting together what she needed for the trip to Maryville. In the meantime, Pa and Diver loaded up traveling supplies: an extra wagon wheel, tools, and a large tarp in case of rain.

The route they'd be taking over Rich Mountain was steep, winding, and extremely rough on both people and vehicles, and Pa knew they'd be spending at least one night alongside the trail each way. Luckily, his big mules were much more intelligent, even tempered, and surefooted, than horses, so Pa figured they'd make the trip just fine.

By early afternoon they'd bid me and Diver farewell and were on their way. I would've liked to of gone along myself, but it wouldn't've been right to saddle Diver with all my chores alongside his own. What I didn't know was Diver had a lot more on his plate than just chores. Him and Forrest had worked out some big plans with Pa. And Delma sendin' that letter when she did was a godsend.

Long about nine o'clock the next mornin', Forrest arrived with a heavy wagon loaded down with lumber, shake shingles, and two kegs of nails.

Pa had decided to build Ma a wide porch across the entire front of the house so she would have somewhere to sit and enjoy the cool evenin' breeze.

"Kate deserves some relaxin' after a hard day in that hot kitchen, or out there in her sun-drenched garden where she spends so much time," he said.

A second wagon, driven by Rolf Schmitt, was close behind with yet more lumber; along with five casement windows, stove pipes, and two brand new, self-standing, wood-burning, cookstoves.

As the wagons came to rest in the front yard Forrest jumped down, and he called Diver over to inspect Rolf's load.

"Got something here even you didn't know about," he said.

He threw back the flaps of a tarpaulin wrapped package, and there sat a beautiful, sixteen-inch-deep copper sink with a drain hole and a wooden stopper in the bottom, and four feet of two-and-a-half-inch copper drainpipe.

"It's wonderful," said Diver admiring the fine craftsmanship. "Where'd you get it?"

"When I asked Orwell about borrowing his freight wagon and told him what it was for, he led me to one of his outbuildings and showed me this sink. He said he'd bought it a few years back for a project he was planning and just never got around to usin' it. He thought Ma would get a lot more use out of it anyway, so he said to take it along. I offered to pay him for it, but he said seeing me and Pa take his brother, Jud, and his no account son, down a-notch-or-two at the Fourth celebration more than covered the cost."

"Yeah, reckon that was a sight," said Diver. "I just hope we get this project done afore Kate and Zeb get back. Zeb figures they'll be a week or so."

"Well, with Pa thinkin' we're just buildin' a front porch and puttin' in a cookstove, and not knowin' a thing about a new kitchen and breezeway, he won't be worried about gettin' back too soon," said Forrest. "He'll figure we'll be done in a day or two."

Diver stood there holdin' on to his suspender's straps and lookin' over the cabin.

"Well, Rolf, Dean, and Pat, live right down the hill and said they'll be here every chance they get," he said. "And you said Chance'll be by after work each day for as long as we need him. So, I reckon we oughta be fine."

Forrest looked at the eave Diver was eyeing.

"And I don't know if you've heard, but Charley Wrightman said she'll make the porch furniture. I hear she's mighty fine with the woodworkin'," he said.

Diver nodded in agreement. "Yeah, that's what I've heard too. What's she gonna be makin'?"

"A bench and two rocking chairs," said Forrest.

Diver thought about that for a bit and nodded his approval.

"I can see it right now," he said. "Kate and Zeb sittin' out here in the shade of the porch just a rockin' side by side. Perhaps Zeb tellin' yer ma 'bout some explot he had back in his youth helpin' ol' Two Hand stay shed o' them Crow Indians that was always after him. And yer ma just a hangin' on every word with her eyes all lit up the way they do when she's all wound up in a story. I'm thinkin, this here porch is gonna be seein' some mighty fine times. And there ain't a soul deserves it more'n your folks. They's some mighty fine people, ya ask me, and I reckon they deserve 'bout all the rest and relaxin' they can get."

Forrest smiled at the selfless nature of the man. Here he stood praising the attributes of Ma and Pa and talkin' 'bout the comfort they deserved. He didn't even realize that he was the catalyst that had drawn this family back together. Why, before he showed up the way he did, Pa had spent more and more time out there in the wilds. His whole being had drifted into that of a hard driven mountain man and it seemed he no longer had time for his own family. Sure, he provided the best he could when it come to food and shelter, but as for love and comfort? It was like he had just drifted more and more into his solitary ways and couldn't find his way back. Only Ma was able to break into that ruff exterior on the rare occasion that Pa let his guard down.

Then, out of nowhere, God sent this stranger. What Pastor Wilson would call a shepard in the wilderness. A guiding light to lead him home. And a gentle spark that reignited the fire in the heart of this family.

As forrest looked at Diver, that is what he saw. Yet Diver somehow didn't see it in himself.

Forrest smiled and patted Diver on the back. "Well, I reckon ain't nobody gonna be sittin' nowhere if we don't get at it," he said.

"That's 'bout how I see it," said Diver.

They got busy unloading the materials next to the house and placing the stoves and stove pipes in the barn until they were needed. One was for Ma's new kitchen and the other was to be stored until they could find time to deliver it to Long Star. Neither of the women had any idea about what they were receiving.

Pa and Forrest had financed Ma's stove and porch out of the gold I had given them, what little was left of the barn money after Pa gave Pastor Wilson a chunk of it for the Cobbs, and what was left of Pa's fur trade profits from last winter.

What Pa didn't know was Forrest and Sarah May had talked it over and were financing the rest.

As for Long Star's stove, Henry was paying for it. He'd been in on the plan from the start.

The first thing Diver and Forrest did was stake out the front porch. It was to be the entire twenty-seven-foot width of the cabin and eight feet deep with a roof above the entire structure and a single step down into the yard.

They then staked out the kitchen adjacent to the back door. It was sixteen-feet-wide by twelve-feet-deep. Both side walls would have casement windows to allow a cooling breeze. And the whole thing would be separated from the house by a six-foot covered breezeway, open on both ends to help keep the cabin cool while cooking on a warm summer's day.

The kitchen would have the free-standing stove in it, along with a chimney cooker using Ma's wrought iron equipment from the old fireplace. Ain't nothin' better than them rod iron hangers for large boiling pots and drying clothes in the winter. It would also have a work counter built along the east wall with the copper sink in it and the copper pipes plumbed out to a French drain leading down to the creek. There'd be a worktable, plenty of shelf space, and a large stone bread oven built into the back wall.

When Pa built the original cabin, the only window had been a small opening in the bedroom. It allowed a view of the wooded side of the yard and gave minor relief from the heat of the day. The three extra windows Forrest had bought were to enlarge the old bedroom window, add a second bedroom window in the front of the house looking out onto the new porch, and put a window in the kitchen overlooking the creek and barn beyond.

Once the dimensions were staked out, the work began. I helped where I could, which started with finding a good supply of large flat stones to use as foundation columns, and smaller flat stones for the fireplace, chimney, and bread oven construction.

I then spent the best part of my days crushing and mixing lime, sand, and gravel with water to make mortar for Rolf as he built the stone features. As it turned out he was quite a mason, though he didn't even know it himself.

By late Friday, they had moved the stove into the new kitchen and had the sink in place with the drain attached, which finished the interior work.

On Saturday, the French drain was dug, lined with flat stones and gravel, and topped off with a small walkin' bridge that Diver made to ease Ma's way to Little Weston's gravesite.

Then Charley arrived with quite possibly the finest looking bench and rocking chairs I've ever seen. They were works of art with delicately carved figurines in the spindles and backs, and the wood all shaped and warped in such a manner that they made you feel like you was just floatin' there in midair when you used 'em.

How a woman with such a rough exterior could do such exquisite work was beyond me.

As I helped Charley arrange her masterpieces on the front porch, I couldn't have been prouder. She placed them just so, to give users the best mountain views Pa's property had to offer. She then lovingly wiped down each piece with the gentlest of touches to assure that not no bit of sawdust or a trace of trail grit remained behind.

"I ain't never seen nothin' so pretty in all my born days," I told her.

She just stood there smilin' a big ol' pearly-toothed smile and wiped a tear from her eye with the sleeve of the men's shirt she was wearin'.

"I'm a thankin' you for them kind words," she said. "I sure hope it does your mama proud. When I caught wind of what y'all were doin' up here for her, I knew I wanted to help. I'm mighty respectin' of your folks, Billy, for the way they've done right by the Cobbs and all. I tried to thank Diver for nursin' ol' Abner and such, but he said there ain't a thing he's done that ain't on account o' what Zeb and Kate done for him. They's some apple shiners in my book, they are, and I wanted to . . . well I felt . . . oh I don't know, I ain't sputtered so many syllables in all my life. I'm just pleased that ya hanker to my furniture and I hope your folks do to."

With that Charley wiped her broad face one more time and climbed aboard Mr. Grear's wagon that she'd parked at the end of the porch.

"Y'all be good, Billy," she said as she snapped her reigns to get she dozing mules to movin'. "And tell your folks I said hay."

She was just enterin' the down slope of the Cove trail when Diver and Forrest rounded the corner of the house.

Lookin' over her shoulder, she waved, and the men waved back.

"She sure left in a hurry," said Forrest. "I wanted to thank her for all her work."

"I reckon she knows how thankful we are," I said. "She's a real fine lady."

With that, I headed for the springhouse to get me some cold sassafras tea.

A dumbfounded Forrest and Diver stood there watchin' Charley go one way and me go the other.

"Whatcha reckon got into him?" Forrest asked.

"I ain't got the faintest," said Diver.

Amazingly, the work was done. And it was finished in the allotted week we figured we had. All there was left to do was to wait for Ma and Pa to get back home.

I kept an eye out all day Sunday, but didn't see a thing; that wasn't no real surprise. Monday; once again, nary a word. By bedtime Tuesday I must admit, I was beginnin' to get a bit worried. Then finally about one in the afternoon on Wednesday, we heard the rattling of the old wagon coming up the hill. As it came into sight, I ran out into the yard waving, and Pa, smiling ear to ear, waved back. Ma sat stunned, her chin hanging down and her pretty, green eyes stretched wide as she took in the sight of her new front porch.

"Oh Zeb," she gasped. "How? It's beautiful. Did you know about this?"

Pa smiled and laughed and hugged Ma. "Of course I knew about it. Me, Forrest, and Diver had this planned long before we heard from Delma. We just had to find a time to do it when you weren't around. When we got that letter; well it was perfect. Though I must say, I did feel kinda bad about leaving all the work to Diver and Forrest. Just look at that porch. It's even better than I had pictured. I owe both of 'em big for this one."

Ma, with her big eyes just a shinin' was holding Pa's arm with her left hand as she slapped it with her right. "Let's get down and go see it," she said as she squirmed around on the wagon bench and let slip a giggle. "I just can't wait."

Pa hopped from the wagon and turned to help Ma down. By then Diver had come amblin' up and placed his hand on my shoulder. We just stood there smilin' and fixin' to watch the show.

Ma's feet had barely touched the ground before she hurried over and gave me a big ol' hug and kissed me on the forehead. Pa, in the meantime, tousled my hair and gave Diver a heartfelt handshake.

"It looks great," he said. "Better than I expected."

Ma grabbed Pa's hand and nearly drug him to the single step of the front porch. I's mighty pleased seein' em standin' there, and then steppin' into that cool shade, hand in hand, like a couple of teenage sweethearts.

"Look at these," Ma said, indicating the porch furniture. "They're beautiful."

Pa went down on one knee and closely examined the finely carved pieces. "This is the work of a master woodsmith," he said as he looked up at Diver with a quizzical look on his face.

"Charley Wrightman," Diver said.

"No," said Pa.

"Who'd've thought it?" said Diver.

Pa smiled and shook his head as he lightly traced the exquisite carvings with his fingers. Then looking up, he noticed the window.

"What's that?" he asked.

"Oh that," said Diver. "That's a window."

Pa looked at him questioningly.

"Well we might have done a bit more than what we discussed. We figured if you didn't like it, we could always take it back out." He scratched his head for a moment. "Well maybe not the windows, seeing's how I'm afraid we may've put a few holes in your cabin."

"A few holes?" asked Pa.

"Yeah, but nothing to speak of," said Diver. "Come in and see."

Pa helped Ma up out of a rocker where she was just a rockin' and a smilin' and running her hands over the smooth linseed oiled wood.

"Let's see what else has been going on since we've been away," he said.

We all followed Diver into the cabin where he directed everyone into the bedroom. He indicated the two bedroom windows that he and Forrest had worked to hard on cutting out.

"We kinda thought having two fully functioning windows in the bedroom would give a nice cross-breeze and with one of them bein' upfront, y'all could see anyone coming into the yard."

"Wonderful," said Ma.

Pa grinned at her, and then at Diver, and gave a silent nod of approval.

"And if y'all will come this way," Diver said, giving an exaggerated swoop of his hand toward the kitchen.

As we followed him in, I was about to burst with anticipation, but somehow managed to keep my composure.

"We had an extra window," he said, "so we lightened up the kitchen and gave y'all, not only fresh air, but a view of the creek also."

Pa was looking out the new window wondering why he hadn't done that years before, when Ma suddenly shouted, "What happened to my fireplace? All my cooking accessories are gone."

Ma and Pa both stared at Diver.

"Well about that," he said. After actin' a bit nervous and all, he smiled and motioned to the closed back door. "I think if y'all go out yonder, the explanation will be clear."

Ma, lookin' kind o' stunned by all the changes and wonderin' what more there could be, took Pa's arm and they stepped to the door.

I'd been a bit surprised that they hadn't questioned that the door was closed before, seein's how we usually left it open in the summer. But I guess with that big window, the room was so bright it didn't seem out of place.

When Pa opened the door, Ma gasped and threw her hand over her mouth.

"Oh Zeb," she cried, as they stepped through the doorway.

I started to follow them, but Diver stopped me.

"Let them enjoy it," he said. "Let 'em explore."

Me and Diver sat at the kitchen table and listened to the excited gasps and squeals as Ma laid eyes on one treasure after another. Pa laughed, and whooped, and cheered her on. He encouraged her to check everything out, and acted like he didn't notice a single item until she discover it on her own.

It was plumb amazing that my own parents were in there actin' like a couple of kids, not fifteen feet from where I was sittin'.

Truth is, it got me downright tickled because in all my years, I'd never seen them have so much fun. I'm tellin' you, my heart swelled so big it down-right hurt. And the next thing I knew, my eyes was just a leakin' tears that washed down over a big sloppy grin that I just couldn't keep off my face. Of course, I didn't try very hard 'cause, to tell ya the truth, I didn't really care.

Diver laughed and squeezed my shoulder, and when I looked up, his cheeks were tear-stained too.

It was a real good day.

NINE

Birds & Bees

WHILE MA AND PA made their exhaustive inspection of the out-kitchen and breezeway, Diver had me run down to the springhouse and fetch a jug of cold sassafras tea.

Though we always tried to keep a jug or two of the standard brew cooling on a small stone ledge where the frigid spring-waters flowed from the hillside, Diver had made this batch up special. He'd seeped the fragrant root in spring water, then added just a hint of honey for flavor, and a few bruised wild mint leaves to give it a refreshing snap. Then he topped it off with a handful of dandelion blossoms and a couple heaping spoons full of sugar swirled in to sweeten the mix. I was getting a bit impatient watchin' the long process but he said it had to sit for a good six hours so all the flavors could mingle. After that he boiled the whole thing until it just began to bubble and then poured the concoction into a large clay jug that he tightly sealed with an apple wood cork. Having placed the jug in the spring to cool for a couple days, he knew it would now be as cold as the crystal-clear water that flowed around it.

He had figured Ma and Pa would camp out somewhere along the rugged trail on Rich Mountain on their return trip. They would probably arrive home hot and tired, and in need of a refreshing drink. To his way of thinkin', nothin' cut the heat and helped soothe the weary bones like a big, cold mug of special-brewed sassafras tea. And sippin' it while rocking in an evening breeze on your new front porch, well, that oughta just top the cake. Can't say I found a lick of fault in that reasonin'.

When the happy couple finally came back in, we all went out onto the front porch with our full mugs of Diver's tea. Me and Diver sat on the beautiful, sturdy, wood bench with a woodland scene carved all along its five-foot backrest, while and Ma and Pa each settled into their superbly fashioned rockers.

"Oh, Diver . . . Billy," Ma said. "I'm so happy I'm about to burst. It's all so beautiful." Her eyes were startin' to well up again and I reckon I was 'bout glowin' with pride.

"I don't see how you got it all done," said Pa. "Or could even afford to do it."

"Well, it certainly wasn't just us," said Diver. "As you know, Forrest was the true drivin' force behind the whole thing. And then we had all kinds of help from Rolf, Dean, Pat, and Chance. Rolf and Billy here did all the stonework."

Ma and Pa both smiled my way, and I felt my ears heat up as an unmanly blush etched across my face.

"And of course, it was Charley Wrightman that made the furniture," he continued.

"As for any extra expense there may've been, you'll hafta talk to Forrest about that. But I can tell ya true, Clarence's clan and Chance all refused to take any pay whatsoever. They said Kate deserves whatever they could do for her, and there ain't a man in the valley they'd rather help out than you, Zeb."

Ma and Pa both displayed a true expression of gratitude on their faces. Neither was comfortable with receivin' help, and yet they were very appreciative.

"Well, I want you to spread the word," Ma said. "Everyone involved in this is in for a mighty fine dinner come Saturday. And be sure Charley hears about it too."

"Did you have a good trip?" asked Diver.

Ma and Pa looked at each other and laughed.

"I'm so ashamed," said Ma. "We got so involved in all of this," she gestured at all the improvement's, then placed her hand on my cheek, "that we didn't even tell you, Billy. You have a new nephew. His name is James Junior, after his father. But Delma says they'll call him Jimmy, or maybe even JJ."

"And Delma's okay?" I asked. (She about raised me, and I missed her somethin' fierce at times.)

"She's doing just fine," Ma said. "The baby arrived the day after we got there, and we stayed 'til Delma was back on her feet and doing good. I think Jim feels he had the worst of it," she looked at Pa, "but that's just how menfolk are sometimes."

Pa didn't say a thing. Just gave a little sideways nod acknowledging what she'd said.

That evenin' Pa helped Ma get the cookstove fired up and ended up standing around talking with her as she made supper.

"I might see about havin' Charley make a couple o' straight-back chairs for in here," he said. "Standin' around watching you work is plumb tiresome."

Ma smiled, "I could probably find somethin' for you to do," she said.

Pa pondered that for a moment, then said, "No, I'm good. I reckon I got the best view in all the mountains right here. I'd sure hate to go and miss out on any of it by doin' something silly like workin'."

Ma smiled to herself and blushed. She couldn't rightly say what had come over the man, but she surely liked it.

At supper that night, Ma said to Pa and Diver, "I been thinking 'bout that old apple orchard where y'all killed that panther."

They both nodded.

"You reckon them old trees might still have enough apples to be useful?"

"I wouldn't be a bit surprised," said Pa, "and right now'd be 'bout the perfect time to pick 'em."

"I got some chores I been lookin' to catch up on," said Diver, "but I reckon iffen I put 'em off for one more day, it won't matter much. Me and Billy can head out there tomorrow and see what we can get." He gave Pa a wink and said, "Reckon it'll take us the whole day though."

The following day, as Diver was strappin' a couple o' woven baskets for apple totin' on that big black mule we called Mac, and I was saddlin' up Joleen, Mary came ridin' into the yard on a beautiful, white and tan, long haired, Shetland pony.

"Hi, Billy," she called, as she waved and rode up to me and Diver.

"Hi, Mary," I replied. "Where'd you get the pony?"

She sat there running her hand through the pony's long mane and said, "My father bought her off Orwell for my birthday. He said Orwell bought a team of show ponies but after the school board talked him into donating one of them for Miss Mellencamp's use, he didn't really know what to do with the other. Dad must have made a good offer, 'cause here I am."

"Well, it's a real fine animal," I said, looking it over with an appraising eye as if I knew the first thing about Shetland ponies. But I could see Mary was mighty pleased by the attention I was givin' her new pony, so I was just as pleased to be givin' it.

About that time Ma came out and spotted us all standin' down by the bridge, near the barn. She came over and handed Diver a flour sack with some ham sandwiches and corn dodgers in it and a jug of water which he strapped on my mule. She then shaded her eyes and looked up.

"Hello, Mary," she said, "that's a beautiful pony you got there."

Now Ma, did know something about Shetland ponies. They were from the Shetland Isles in the north of Scotland, and anything Scottish was Ma's pleasure.

"Thank you, Mrs. Banion," Mary said. "My father bought her from Orwell for my birthday. Her name is Fancy."

"Well, that's nice," said Ma, "I can see where her name came from. Happy birthday."

"Thank you," said Mary as she patted Fancy's jaw. "I just wanted to come by and show her to Billy since he wasn't at church on Sunday."

"Yes, Billy was pretty busy buildin' me a new house," Ma said as she indicated the new porch.

Mary looked in astonishment at the house, and then at me.

"You did that?" she said.

"Aw shucks," I said, feeling that pestersome heat once more rising in my cheeks. I kicked the toe of my shoe in the dirt as I said, "It wasn't all me. I had help."

Out of the corner of my eye, I saw Diver grin and nonchalantly cover his mouth as if he was yawning.

As Mary sat there with a kind of admiring look on her face, Diver recovered and said, "I've got an idea. Why don't you two go pick them apples. That way I can get my tasks done. Whatcha think Kate?"

I saw a flash of concern cross Ma's face. At first, I thought it was worry that there could be another panther, but then I saw her give Mary a quick glance.

What was that for? I wondered.

Then, after the slightest of pauses, she shook her head and said, "That sounds like fun."

Looking at me and Mary, she said, "You two have a good time and get me lots of apples."

"What do you say?" I asked Mary.

"Oh yes," she said, soft and shy-like, "let's go."

I saw that flash in Ma's eyes again, and thought, *I don't know what it is with womenfolk and I guess I never will.*

Anyway, I figured if we was goin', we best get at it, so as soon as Diver swapped the apple baskets to Joleen, I climbed aboard and with a click of my tongue headed down the barely visible trail that Diver said would lead to the old orchard.

As we rode away, Diver said to Ma, "Tell Zeb that corn has all pollinated, and is husking out just fine, but I'm gonna go check on the irrigation system. Reckon I'll be all day if he asks."

It was a pleasant journey, that late July morning, as we trailed through an old growth forest that eventually led us to a meandering little brook just as Diver had told me it would. My big mule had no trouble crashing through and stomping down the underbrush, thereby clearing the way for Mary and her pony.

At the brook, we turned left and plodded straight up the center of the stream until we came to a six-foot-high beaver dam blocking the way. Beyond the dam was a small pond of open water and a large swampy area that spread far off into a forested mountain valley, covering underbrush, and swirling around a great corps of dead or dying trees.

At the dam, our route was to circle around a large round-topped rock protruding from the ground with a flat face on the brook side and a gentle slope on the other. Then by simply passing through a hundred acres or so of relatively open ground beneath towering pine trees, we would reach our destination. All in all, it was an unadventurous and enjoyable trip.

When we entered the meadow that the orchard occupied, it was like riding into another world. Flowers were everywhere. Small, dainty puffs of white sprinkled the field like snowflakes, covering the thick growths of tall fescue and Indian grass. Stout, narrow sprigs adorned with tiny, yellow, bell-shaped flowers swayed in the light breeze. Blues, reds, and pinks all competed to dazzle the eye as if a master painter had finally accomplished his lifelong masterpiece.

Black and yellow bees buzzed from blossom to blossom and butterflies flittered around on yellow-orange wings outlined with black markings. Some had nearly translucent blue wings and coal black bodies, while others floated around on large yellow wings of the softest velvety texture and blended in perfectly with the sun facing flowers.

Here and there darted multicolored dragonflies who's rapidly beating quartet of glistening wings seemed to disappear when they took flight, only to reappear in a shimmering blaze of translucent colors when they gently settled on a jewelweed twig or a Little Bluestem blade.

All of this color and activity, along with hundreds of apples, both dangling and dropped, blushing in shades of greens, yellows, reds, and browns, made the clearing a truly otherworldly site.

"Oh, Billy, it's beautiful," said Mary as she hopped down from Fancy's back and ran her hand through a large patch of delicate white and pink wood sorrel.

I climbed down from Joleen and stood next to her gazing out across the wonderland.

"I'll never forget it," Mary said. "Oh, thank you. Thank you so much." And with that she reached over and kissed me—right on the cheek.

Well, I'll tell ya, I went completely numb. I couldn't even breath. I was afraid I was gonna pass out right there on the spot and make a total fool of myself. Mary Wilson had kissed me on the cheek. My very first kiss. I mean, you can't count Ma and Delma and Sarah May. They're family, and women kinfolk gettin' all mushy and stuff is something you just naturally gotta put up with.

But Mary. That kiss from Mary wasn't nothin' like one from Ma. It somehow lingered there all warm and wonderful, and I figured it was just about the best feelin' I ever felt. Maybe even better than when I first noticed I could see Henry when we were stuck in that dark cave with no light.

It's hard to explain, but I reckon in my young mind I figured that kiss was just about the best thing that could ever happen to a fella.

Finally, when I realized I could breathe again, I looked over at Mary. She was standing with her hands clasped behind her back, looking down at her feet as if she was sort of embarrassed. I smiled at her. Well, she glanced up and she smiled right back. In the old odes and songs, they talk about being smitten, and that's just what I was. I was plumb smitten.

"I guess we should get some apples for your ma," Mary said, nodding at the apple trees.

Her shimmering blond hair was slightly blowin' in a light breeze, and her clear blue eyes held me transfixed. As marvelous and beautiful as that glade of flowers was, it held nothing on Mary.

I looked around as I came out of my daze, and realized I'd done forgotten what we were there for.

"Reckon you're right," I said.

For the next couple of hours, we had a grand ol' time pickin' Ma's apples.

I reckon we could've been done a lot sooner, but Mary kept actin' like she was startled, and scared, every time she came across an apple worm, or a stinging caterpillar; and I kept actin' like I wasn't, and rushed over to save her.

Course, there wasn't nothin' to them apple worms, but if you've ever been stung by a Saddleback caterpillar you know you don't ever wanta be stung by one again. Them things hurt.

By the time we had both filled our pickin' baskets for the sixth or seventh time and emptied them into the big woven baskets strapped on Joleen, it was gettin' downright hot under that early afternoon sun.

"What say we take a break," I said, as I placed my basket on the ground next to Mary's. "I reckon we done got every plump apple worth havin' in this whole orchard."

Mary smiled, and nodded. Then to my surprise, and absolute pleasure, she took my hand.

We strolled across the colorful meadow to where Joleen and Fancy were tied in the shade near a bunch of pine trees. I tossed the pickin' baskets on top the collected apples strapped on Joleen's sides and patted her neck as I loosened the lunch sack and water jug Ma had prepared.

"This is a mighty pretty place to picnic," I said.

Mary smiled as she looked around and nodded.

Pointing toward the brook I said, "Why don't we sit over yonder."

When we came to the large rock we had rounded near the brook, I helped Mary up the gently sloping side until we stood on top.

The flat face of the rock was overlooking the small pond and the wending swamp below, and from our vantage point we could see a family of mallard ducks slowly gliding undisturbed across the shallow, crystal, water.

"It's perfect," said Mary.

We soon found a nice, shaded spot with a smooth flat rock just large enough for the two of us to sit on while we enjoyed our lunch.

As we ate, we watched a couple of active beavers and laughed at their antics.

They were busy swimming in and out of the swamp, dragging sections of tree trunks and limbs that seemed much too long for them to handle. Yet, as we watched, they worked the branches into the fabric of the dam as if there was nothin' to it. I suppose to them there wasn't, but I was mystified.

Pretty soon, three beaver pups came crawlin' up the side of the dam and found a muddy, but sunny spot, that they stopped to wrestle in.

Then, I caught a movement out of the corner of my eye. Watching closely, a shadow in the underbrush magically transformed into a slinking fox.

I pointed it out to Mary as it slowly glided through the brush below. It was obviously tryin' to sneak up on the pups hopin' for an easy meal.

Mary tensed up and was just about to yell out a warning, when suddenly, there was a loud clap in the water. It was the father beaver slapped his tail on the pond's surface to alert his family before he dove below.

At the sound, the mother quickly scrambled up the dam and drove her pups below.

In no time at all, the fox was left trottin' along the shoreline all alone. When he realized there was no lunch to be had, he slunk off into the deep brush to try his luck elsewhere.

As we sat there, we watched several colorful finches flittering through the trees. At one point, a butterfly floated down and alit on Mary's hand. She gently raised it up and caressed its lifted wings against her cheek. It was a beautiful sight.

I believe I could have been content just stayin' right there for the rest of my days. But then looking down again, I noticed a shadow spreadin' across the pond. I shaded my eyes and looked at the sky.

"Them's rain clouds," I said reluctantly. "We better be getting back."

Mary looked and said, "I guess you're right, but I sure do hate to leave."

"I do too," I said. "But maybe we can return some day."

"Oh, I hope so," said Mary. "This was the best day I've ever had. Thank you, Billy. I'll never forget it."

Then she stretched over and gave me a little peck right on the lips. *Right on the lips.* Remember, I said that kiss on the cheek was about the best feelin' a fella could ever have? I was wrong.

TEN

Hand Me Downs

A SLOW DRIZZLE BEGAN TO FALL as we left the brook and entered the old growth forest. As the rain gradually intensified, we were often sheltered by the thick canopy above. We hurried as much as possible, trying to beat the worst of the storm, but I had to be careful to rein back on Joleen as her long-legged stride could easily outdistance that of Fancy.

All in all, it was an uneventful though quite wet trek and by midafternoon we finally entered the homestead and hurried to the house.

I left a thoroughly waterlogged Mary standing on the porch as I led Fancy and Joleen across the bridge and into the barn.

"Appear to be a might wet," said Diver.

He was standing in the breezeway between the tool storage area and the stock pen.

"Yeah, rain'll do that to ya," I said.

He chuckled and said, "Reckon so. Where's that pretty little gal you rode off with?"

"I left her on the porch, while I got the animals out of the rain."

Diver came over and examined a couple of the apples, before nodding and placing them back in the basket.

"Nice looking crop," he said. "You run and take care of your little lady. I'll unload these and get the team ready to go. I reckon Kate is gonna want me or Zeb to take her home. She'll never let her head out in this rain on her own"

I looked at Diver and kinda mumbled, "She ain't 'My Lady'."

"What's that?" asked Diver.

He could hear me just fine and I knew it. He was just fishin' and tryin' to rile my dander. I think a bit o' Pa was rubbin' off on him, just the same as he was rubbin' off on Pa.

"Aw, nothin'," I said, not givin' him the satisfaction.

"Well, tell your ma I'll have the team hitched up, and that little pony tied behind the wagon. I got a tarp

Mary can wrap up in that'll keep her as dry as possible while I get her home."

I noticed he called her Mary that time . . .

"I'll be watching out, so when she's ready just give a wave from the porch, and I'll bring the team around," he said.

I nodded and waved, before trotting out the big open door and through the growing rivulets of water that were forming on the muddy embankment leading down to the bridge.

As I crossed the swiftly flowing stream, I noticed Pa scramblin' through the muck toward his tannin' shed. So much for Ma's and Pa's whole day together.

The rain wasn't all that bad but didn't look as if it would be easing up anytime soon. After jumpin' a large puddle that had formed at the end of the rain-slick bridge, I sloshed through the front yard and noticed Mary was no longer on the porch. Ma must have invited her in.

Stoppin' to stomp my feet a bit and shake out my clothes under the protection of the new porch roof, I tried to knock off as much rainwater as possible. Before the porch was built, we had no choice but to charge on in with water runnin' off our backs, but I figured Ma wouldn't look real kindly on that now.

When I entered the cabin, I saw Mary leaning forward in the kitchen with her long, wet hair hangin' down from the right side of her face, as she vigorously dried it with Ma's favorite towel.

She turned her head my way and smiled. Even soakin' wet, she was a mighty pretty gal.

"Where's Ma?" I said.

"Oh, she said she was gonna find somethin' for me to wear. She should be right out."

I didn't rightly know what Ma could find, seein's how Mary was only half her size, but knowing Ma, I knew she'd come up with somethin'.

We spent a few minutes awkwardly standin' around, kinda not knowin' what to talk about now that we were home. Then Ma opened her bedroom door and beckoned for Mary to enter.

"I've got some dry clothes for you lying on the bed, and a fresh towel to dry off with," she said. "Go on in and change, and I'll warm up some cedar tea."

As Mary went into Ma's room, Ma turned to me and said, "And you, young man, better scoot on up to your room and get dried off your own self."

"Sure Ma," I said, as I grabbed the threadbare towel that she offered me.

Yeah, I noticed Mary was offered the best we had, and I got a rag not much better than burlap, but I didn't mind. I guess girls will stick together.

I was back down in the kitchen in no time. Of course, workin' with that old bare towel I was only half dried off, but I was freshly dressed in my only spare pair of trousers and an old pullover leather shirt that was a hand-me-down from Cassey.

When Mary came out of Ma's room, she was dressed in some of my old clothes that I'd outgrown. I reckon Ma must have kept them for quilting work or the like. I'd never seen a girl in boy's clothes before but make no mistake about it; she looked a whole lot better in em than I ever had.

She was standing there with a slight flush on her face, rubbing her arms and clinching her hands in the soft fabric, and looking a bit uncomfortable, but not in the least unhappy.

As for me, I just couldn't take my eyes off her.

It was then that Ma came in from the outer kitchen with two mugs of hot tea. She paused for a moment, her eyes flicking back and forth between us, then settled herself and handed each of us a mug.

"Drink this," she said. "It'll take the chill off." Then she looked Mary over.

"I think that'll do," she said. "There shouldn't be many people out in this rain. We'll wrap you up good, so you don't get soaked again, and I don't think anyone will notice the clothes."

"Diver's got a tarp to cover her in," I said.

"Well, I'd prefer something cleaner, but I guess it'll do," said Ma. "Is he gettin' the wagon?"

"Yeah, he said he'd keep an eye out. Just wave when she's ready and he'll bring it around."

Ma nodded. "Well, you two drink your tea now. When you're done, I'll wave for Diver."

Ma went about her business. She wiped up the damp spots we'd left on the kitchen floor and she found a gunny sack to put Mary's wet clothes in. As she worked, she asked us about our day, and if we'd got her some good apples and such.

I noticed Mary kept rubbing her hand on my old clothes with a soft grin on her face, and somehow that gave me a warm feeling inside. I had a hard time concentrating on what Ma was saying, and after she queried about the trek through the rain for the third time, she shook her head and gave up.

"I reckon it's about time to wave for Diver," she said, as she stepped out the front door.

When Diver pulled up in the front yard with Fancy tied behind the wagon, he jumped down and carried a small freight tarp onto the porch. Being wrapped up in a heavy coat against the long, wet drive ahead of him, he looked about twice his normal size.

"I reckon this should keep the young lady dry," he said, handing the tarp to Ma.

Ma flicked it out and looked it over, checkin' for bugs or spiders, I suppose.

"Yeah, it looks like it'll do," she said as she wrapped the linseed oil and wax infused cloth around Mary and over her head. "Now, you be sure and say hi to your pa for us and tell him we'll see him at church come Sunday," she said to Mary."

"I sure will," said Mary.

Ma kissed her on the cheek and handed the gunny sack of wet clothes to Diver.

"Okay, Miss Mary, let's be on our way," he said.

Mary tried to follow Diver, but wrapped in that bulky tarp, she couldn't move. Diver glanced back and saw the problem.

"Don't you fret none, little lady," he said. "I got ya."

He then picked her up and carried her to the wagon.

"Bye," I shouted as he sat her on the bench and crawled up alongside of her.

Mary reached one small hand up and wiggled her fingers between the tarp and her chin. "Bye," she called back. "I sure had a good time."

With that Diver drove the team out of the yard and down the Cove trail. I watched until they were out of sight.

"You really like that girl, don't ya," said Ma.

"Well, yeah, she's all right," I said reaching up and scratching the back of my neck.

Ma grinned. "All right, huh?" she said.

As she turned to go into the house, she stopped and kissed me on the cheek and said, "I reckon she thinks you're 'all right' too."

Even hearing Ma say it made me feel all warm and fuzzy inside. Being 'all right' to Mary Wilson; that was about all I could think about right then.

When Diver returned, the rain was still falling though it hadn't really intensified. There was a steady patter on the roof and the creek had become a bit swifter and muddier, but it didn't appear to be too threatenin' yet. I'd seen it when it was a swift moving torrent and that was a long way off.

In the distance we could hear the soft rumble of thunder that gradually drew nearer as we ate our supper. Before long, the sky darkened, and Pa lit our lanterns. To tell the truth, I thought it was a pleasant evening. We cleared the dishes and sat around talkin' and playin' checkers as the kitchen window glowed occasionally with far off lightning.

Then suddenly, the window lit up like midday and a deafenin' crack and boom exploded across the room.

"That was a close one," said Diver. "Reckon I oughta get home while I can."

"Why don't you stay here tonight?" said Ma.

"No, I'll be fine," said Diver. "It's just with this kind o' storm, it's likely to get worse before it gets better, so I better get to movin'."

"Well, if you insist," said Ma, lookin' at Pa with worry on her face.

"He'll be fine," said Pa.

We all followed Diver out the front door and stood on the porch as he wrapped himself in the big coat he had worn when he took Mary home.

"See y'all in the morning," he shouted over the cacophony of falling rain and rumblin' thunder. He then tucked his chin low and holding down his hat with his right hand while grasping his closed collar with his left, he made a dash for the barn.

I thought he was gonna slip and slide under the railing on the bridge, but he caught himself in time and made it safely home.

In a flash of lightning, we saw him wave and we waved back. Then we went inside, and I started washing dishes for Ma as she and Pa played one last game of checkers.

"Reckon we may as well go to bed," she said, conceding the last few moves to Pa.

It was a bit early, but not enough to speak about, so I said goodnight and climbed up to my loft. In the darkness, I ran my hand through the soft hair of my panther skin rug on the wall and felt a small shiver down my back. I just stood there in the dark brushing that pelt and listenin' to the rain on the roof.

I then laid down on my feather mattress and closed my eyes, reliving the sight of Mary as she reveled in that meadow of multi-colors. How she laughed at the antics of the beaver family, and tensed up with fear when I pointed out that fox sneakin' up on the frolicking beaver pups. It was a magical day.

I always did enjoy sleepin' during a thunderstorm, and as I laid there in the dark thinking about Mary and listening to the rain drumming on the shakes of the roof, I gradually drifted off into a contented sleep.

ELEVEN

Tempest

BAM, BAM, BAM . . . bam, bam, bam. I sat straight up in my bed when a loud pounding on the front door tore me from sleep.

"Zeb! . . . Zeb! get up."

It was Diver calling, but I could barely make out his strained voice over the driving rain.

"Zeb!"

"Hold on a minute. Let me get a lantern lit." I heard Pa's voice carry through the cabin.

A few moments later, I saw a glow appear in the access hole to my loft. It softly lit the ceiling above and caused a skeletal effect as it outlined the top few rungs of my protruding ladder. I then heard the storm intensify and recede as the front door opened and closed. The dim light then crept across my ceiling and nearly faded away as the lantern was carried to the table in the back part of the kitchen.

"What's the problem?" I heard Pa ask.

"I been up half the night watchin' this storm," Diver said. "It ain't slowed up for a minute. The creek is rising, and I figure by daybreak it'll be out of its banks."

By this time, I was out of bed and climbing down the ladder.

"I don't reckon it can reach the barn or cabin," said Pa. "There's a lot of slope downstream."

"No, I'd say the homestead is sittin' fine," said Diver. "It's the corn I'm worried about."

I had just walked in and sat by the table trying to wipe the grit from my eyes as Pa put his big bare foot on the bench and said, "You thinkin' that hillside'll get so saturated it'll give way?"

"I can't see it holding," said Diver, "unless we close all those irrigation flume gates and get that water flowing around the field."

"Reckon that'll do it?" said Pa.

"Ain't got no choice," said Diver. "Either it'll hold, or it won't."

"Okay," said Pa. "Throw what you think we'll need into the wagon and hitch up the team. I'll get dressed and meet you in the barn."

As Driver headed back out into the pouring rain, Pa scratched his belly through his baggy long johns and hurried into his bedroom to get dressed, I sat there at the table wondering what mortal men could do in the middle of such a storm. It was a horrifying prospect to me, but I reckon sometimes a man has just got to buck-up and do what must be done.

When Pa came back out o' his room with Ma close behind I asked, "You want me to get dressed and come along?"

Pa shook his head and pulled on his hunting shirt and tricorn hat. "Not this time, son," he said.

Ma came over and hugged me to her breast.

"We'll have some coffee and a hot breakfast waiting on you when you get back," she told Pa.

"No hurry," he said. "I reckon we'll be awhile. Why don't you two go on back to bed and get some sleep. I'll wake you if we get back before you're up."

We all knew she wouldn't be goin' back to bed, but Ma just smiled as she kissed him and said, "You be careful out there."

"Ain't never anything but," he said with a smile, before headin' out into the dark pounding rain.

The way Pa and Diver later told it, they had quite a time that night. When Pa got to the barn, Diver had already tossed several tools, boards, and nails, into the wagon and was in the process of hitching up the team. Pa joined in and they were soon on their way through the slashing rain with lightning rippling across the night sky like great blue and white spider webs. The thunder rumbled and rolled across the mountains with an occasional crack accompanied by a slash of brilliance illuminating the countryside all around.

Both men knew they were blessed to have steely nerved mules pulling the wagon. Horses would have bolted at the first thunderclap and been totally useless in such a tempest.

Arriving at the small corps of pines below the ridge where the beehive rested, they stopped as far from the massive hardwoods as possible.

It was best to avoid the threat of any widowmakers that may hang above.

Pa swung the wagon around to place the mules' tails to the wind and to let the wagon give the team some protection from the elements. They were a good team and he wanted to give them the consideration they deserved.

After cramming nails and hammers into their pockets and grabbing as many boards, stakes, and shovels as they could carry, they began sloshing their way up the gentle, but slippery slope of the muddy field.

Water cascaded around their ankles and pulled at their sodden pant legs. Slippin' and slidin', they plowed on through the muck and slowly made their way, yard by yard, toward the crest of the hill. At times they were bent nearly horizontal to the rise trying to keep their purchase as the whipping wind blasted them with sheets of cold, penetrating rain.

Amazingly, it appeared the sturdy stalks were holding their own. As far as Pa could tell, none were on the ground.

Long green corn leaves whipped and snapped around in the swirling winds, slashing like sabers and Pa and Diver both soon had bloodied hands, necks and faces.

The boards they carried tangled in the swaying stalks, and the shovels more than once tripped them, as the long handles worked their way between their legs or under their feet, sending first one and then the other to the muddy ground.

It was as if every foot of advancement was a trial of endurance, and every element in nature was trying to impede their progress.

How the corn was even standing was nothing short of a miracle at that point.

Finally making it to the top, they immediately began closing open gates and clearing clogged drainages. Here and there a gate had torn lose, or a section of flume had washed out. They wasted no time pounding new boards home and nailing them in place.

With each repair, less water escaped the upper flumes and was diverted over a nearby hillside, but the on-rush was quickly rising in the lower sections. Rushing water from a higher elevation lapped at the very tops of the boards. Unless something was done soon, the entire irrigation system would fail.

"What do we do now?" screamed Pa into Diver's ear trying to be heard over the lashing rain and flailing wind-swept trees and vegetation.

Diver thought for a second and then pointed farther up the rise into the thick timber. Pa nodded and they both used their shovels to help them keep their footing as they climbed around massive boulders and gnarled trees trying to find a sheltered spot where they could hear one another.

After several minutes of blindly stumbling through the unforgiving elements, they found what they were looking for.

Huddled close on the leeward side of a large boulder, they could finally talk.

"We need to get up to where I diverted this irrigation stream off the main brook," Diver shouted. "If we can find a way to block it and force the flow down the main channel, we just might save the crop yet."

Pa nodded and indicated for Diver to lead the way. It was a relatively short, but ankle-twisting trek up to the mainstream. Even in the pouring rain, Pa could see as they climbed that the water flowed along a natural course. It spread and narrowed in places yet gathered into a single branch before it entered the flumes. How Diver had managed to find and utilize this providential causeway was beyond him.

At the mainstream of what Pa thought might be a fork of Vinegar Creek, he saw that Diver had dug a small channel out of the corner of a bend and built a stone berm which created a pressure point that forced water over the lowered edge of the stream-bank. From there, it was gravity fed all the way to his irrigation system. Under normal function, it delivered a steady, but manageable flow. But excessive rainwater from the storm had ripped open the narrow channel and released a torrent of water.

"Brilliant," Pa yelled. "How do we close it?"

"I don't know," Diver yelled back. "I built it with a gate, but it's all washed out."

"Let's see if we can block it." Pa screamed. His words were ripped away by the storm's furor.

He picked up rocks and began heaving them into the cut out. Diver joined in. Rock after rock was thrown into the turbulence only to be swept away by the powerful current. They quickly realized what they were doing was to no avail.

Diver grabbed Pa's shoulder and waved his hand to stop him. With his mouth close to Pa's ear, he shouted, "Not working. We hafta try somethin' else."

Pa straightened up, nodded, spread his arms, and shrugged.

Diver looked around for a solution. There had to be a way! Then he saw it.

"There!" he yelled and pointed.

Pa looked where Diver was pointing. It was the tangled mess of an ancient logjam, perhaps fifty yards upstream from where the irrigation channel was. He then studied the stream bank from the logjam to the bend where Diver's channel was and instantly knew what Diver had in mind. He nodded agreement in and waved Diver on.

In the rain, it wasn't easy to get a grip on the slick, water-soaked logs, but after a few slips and shoves, they finally had one in the flow. It bobbed down the raging stream before slammimg into the large rocks at the bend, only to spin out into the current and race out of sight. The second log tapped off the bank before reaching the bend, swirled around, and crashed into the gravel bar beyond the channel. It was of no use. But the third attempt, payed off.

There was a large section of a blown-down tree with several limbs attached to it already resting in the water. Twisting and flailing in the stream, it only needed a little help to get started on its journey.

First, they used their shovels to slash and chop it free from some clinging vines and limbs. Then, when it shifted and was close to breaking free from its final restraints, they teamed up to pry it loose. With a final heave and the snapping of limbs the tree broke its bonds and rushed down stream. It was only through the greatest of care that neather of the men were swept away with it.

At last, they had found the perfect trajectory into the channel opening and with the splintered of limbs and the force of the current it lodged firm and held in place.

"Hurry," Pa yelled, "We hafta secure it."

Sloshin' back down to the bend, Pa and Diver quickly began pitchin' stones into the space around the tree. In no time at all, the flow of water was blocked, and the tree was locked in so tight they figured it would not become dislodged. They then sat down in the pourin' rain and caught their breath.

When they got back down to the flume, they watched as the water level dropped. A little cleanout of the main ditch let the water bypass the gates and spill over a nearby ledge and harmlessly spread through the forest below.

Having accomplished everything they could, they loaded up the wagon and headed back to the barn. If the crop washed away or survived, it was out of their hands at that point.

By the time they made it back it was still raining, but the lightning and thunder had receded into the distance, and the winds had slowed considerably.

At home, Ma and I heard the rattle of the wagon. We stepped out onto the porch to see them pull into the barnyard just as the skies began to lighten up in the east. Coffee was on, and the cookstove was heated, so Ma hurried back in to start cooking breakfast. She knew it wouldn't take long for the men to take care of the team and come in, in search of some warm vittles.

They'd had a hard night.

TWELVE

Diver's Proposition

BY MID-MORNING, the rain had slowed to an intermittent drizzle. A lazy mist hung over the mountains creating a somewhat hollow affect in its tranquility. No longer did the nerve-grating disturbances of raging winds and pounding sheets of driven rain numb the senses. The ear-splitting crash of exploding thunder that had ripped apart the swollen skies had slowly drifted into the far distances and gradually ceased.

In their stead was left a countryside cloaked in a cocoon of silence. An unnatural absence of sound. It was as if nature had paused from its rage and fury to calm its wrath, to take a breath.

In this nearly spectral world of misty gloom and muted sound, I strolled across our grounds looking at the scattered damage. A dead limb had crashed down near Ma's chicken coop grazing its roof and walls with brittle twigs, but no extensive damage was done.

Ma's garden had been pounded flat in the deluge but with most of the early plantings near the end of their producing life, and the late season vegetables still young enough to recover well before they matured, the loss was minimal.

Pa's tanning shed, being the outbuilding nearest to the creek, had been swept away along with all the materials he had inside it. Over the next few days, I found a few of his leather working tools downstream, but most of his equipment had to be remade by Diver or himself.

Pa had recently sold last year's fur harvest to pay for Ma's porch and stove, so very little of his trapping and hunting revenue had been lost.

Unfortunately, our springhouse had partially flooded, destroying all our buttermilk, ten gallons of our fresh milk, and six pounds of butter. Everything else was high enough up on the shelves to be left untouched. And seein's how Tilly would soon replace the milk and butter, all in all, we faired pretty well.

The cabin, barn, smokehouse, outhouse, and root cellar came through the storm fine.

By early afternoon, the skies cleared, and the swollen creek receded into a rapidly flowing, slightly enlarged version of its normally gentle self.

Diver loaded up a sack of tools and putting reins on old Mac, jumped on bareback to go inspect the cornfield while me and Pa cleaned up the refuse left by the storm. We soon learned there would be no shortage of firewood that year.

By suppertime Diver had returned, and he told us what he'd discovered while we ate.

"The corn came through the night better than it had any right to," he said, shakin' his head and looking at Pa. "And I reckon its largely due to the failure of my poorly designed irrigation system."

He had Pa's full attention at that. Pa knew Diver's irrigation system was a miraculous feat of engineering and he didn't understand why the man was berating himself.

"You see," Diver continued, "each ditch between the rows of corn was built with a series of stopgaps in the form of small dirt berms across the channel. I should have used wooden baffles, but I figured dirt berms would work just fine. The idea was to slow the water down and give it time to soak into the ground instead of it all runnin' off."

"Sounds reasonable," Pa said.

"And it would have been too," said Diver. "Under normal conditions, but as you know, them weren't no normal conditions last night. That torrent of water that came washin' down them ditches before we got the flumes fixed at the top of the field washed every last one of them berms out. And them washed out berms is what allowed that floodwater to sweep on down them ditches, and flow into the forest below, without taking the corn with it."

"Ain't that somethin'," mused Pa.

"It sure is," said Diver. "And then, when we repaired the flumes up top, it slowed the waterflow enough to keep excessive erosion from undermining the crops and washing them out anyway."

Pa nodded his head, and said, "And if it weren't for you wakin' me up in the dead o' the night, we'd a lost the whole lot."

"Can't be givin' me too much credit for that," said Diver. "I never could sleep much in a heavy storm. And, as for that corn withstanding them winds; well I reckon we got the Almighty to thank for that."

"Can't argue with that," Pa said, as he reached over and squeezed Ma's hand.

"After inspecting the field," Diver continued, "I repaired them broken flume gates, and then climbed back up to the main creek and reopened a small irrigation channel. Next time, iffen a next time ever comes, I figure that blown-down tree with all those limbs juttin' out and all locked down in place with them stones will make it a whole lot easier to block the extra flow."

When we gave thanks that night, there was no shortage of things to be thankful for. Unfortunately, as we were to soon learn, much of the Cove had not faired quite as well as we had.

Come Sunday mornin,' when we loaded up and headed to church, it didn't take long to see great swaths of destruction across the fertile fields of the Cove. All along the brooks and creeks, standing water still covered washed-out fields. In places, Abrams Creek was several times its normal width, and it had small islands of brush and debris swirling in the current as it headed somewhere farther downstream.

Barns and outbuildings laid crumpled in the fields. Others were left shattered and splintered, hanging where they'd been discarded in the limbs of broken, leafless trees. The slightly raised roadway accessing Abrams Creek Bridge stood mere inches above the standing water that stretched far out into the fields on both sides. The bridge itself was still sound, but large erosion ditches were etched out along the edges of the on and off ramps, and they would need immediate attention

Upon crossing the bridge and climbing to the top of a rise, Pa pulled the team to a stop when we gained a clear view of the valley before us. Stretched far off into the distance, the normally bountiful fields of corn and beans laid twisted and flattened, as if some great hand had reached down from the heavens and stirred the very fabric of the earth.

Great swaths of destruction stretched out for hundreds, perhaps thousands of acres. Even the occasional fields fortunate enough to be above the reach of the rising waters had been decimated by the swirling winds.

The devastation defied comprehension and it was an awestruck and saddened Banion Clan that pulled into the churchyard that morning.

Before the regular service, Pastor Wilson shared a community bulletin to fill us all in on the state of the Cove.

"As you all know," he began, "we had a devastating flood this week. Many people throughout the community need our help and our prayers. Please be as generous with your bounty and your time as you can. As for the damages, I will share what I know.

"First off, we can give thanks to the Lord that there were no deaths." This was followed by a chorus of, "Amens," and "Praise the Lords."

"There were losses of more than a dozen cows, at least two horses, and an untold number of goats, pigs, chickens, and sheep. In fact, Sister Agnes lost her entire flock of chickens to a lightning strike.

"Volunteer work crews have been formed to repair roads, bridges, outbuildings, and about a half a dozen homes.

"Crop damages were extreme. Orwell says he's lost at least a third of his corn, not to mention a huge loss of beans and tobacco. Some of the smaller farmers have lost their entire year's harvest.

"We've had riders come through from Tuckaleechee, Wear's Cove, and Sevierville, all claiming they were hit just as bad, if not worse than we were. They're trying to buy grain commitments at top dollar to see them through the winter. Corn will surely be at a premium, and you can rest assured each community is going to be lookin' out for themselves. For now, the best we can do is to be aware of the needs of others and help our neighbors as best we can.

"Please stand and bow your heads for prayer."

After a prayer for those in need, and of thanks for those who were spared the worst of the deluge, Pastor Wilson took the pulpit.

With that, he opened his Bible and spoke about the trials and tribulations of Job. How in life, sometimes it seems every hand is turned against us. Every misfortune comes our way. Gloom and despair seem to be our only companions. And yet, God is in control. If we trust in the Lord, He will see us through.

It was a thoughtful and timely sermon, but throughout, I'm ashamed to say, I could only ponder two things. Mary sat on the front pew and had not once glanced back my way. And Miss Melloncamp was nowhere to be seen.

The question of Mary could easily be explained by the fact that she was perched directly below her father's gaze. Did that have anything to do with our little adventure at the orchard, I wondered?

But, for a schoolmarm to miss church? Other than a major illness, it just did not happen.

After service, we stood around near our wagon talkin' with Forrest and Sarah May, 'til Pastor Wilson strolled up. He shook hands with Forrest, Pa, and Diver, and politely acknowledged Sarah May before turning to Ma.

"I wanted to thank you for looking after my Mary the other day," he said, while handing Ma a cloth wrapped package. "This is the clothes you so kindly lent her."

Ma quickly took the package, and handed it to Pa.

"I'm sorry I didn't have a dress for her to wear," she told the pastor in a lowered voice, as she glanced around not wanting to be overheard. "I'm afraid once Delma married and moved to Maryville, all her childhood clothes were used for quiltin' and patchwork."

"No worry," said Pastor Wilson. "You were most gracious in your help. And sending her wrapped up as you did against prying eyes? Well, the discretion was much appreciated. I just can't thank you enough. You know, there are those who question the abilities of a widower to raise a girl on his own. Even in the best of congregations, tongues do tend to wag. But my Mary is my shining light, and I just couldn't bear to live without her."

Ma was nodding her head as she took his hand in both of hers.

"She's a wonderful girl," said Ma.

"Oh, I couldn't agree more," said Sarah May, who had been standing next to Ma and listening to the conversation. "She's a testament to her father. And I, for one, wouldn't let anyone say different."

"She's is a wonderful daughter," Pastor Wilson continued, "but I'm afraid at times, she does show a lack of judgment. Like riding out to your place Kate, without telling me. She scared me half to death when that storm came up and I didn't know where she was."

Ma nodded in sympathy.

"I don't know what I'd have done if something had happened to her."

Everyone in the Cove was aware that after losing his wife in childbirth, Pastor Wilson had given up his first ministry in Knoxville and turned his unnamed daughter over to his parents in Trenton, New Jersey.

He had then spent three long years wallowing in self-pity, working as a farmhand near Nashville. During that time, his health had deteriorated and by all appearances, he didn't care if he lived or died.

Then finally, with a tortured mind and broken body, he somehow found his way back to his parents' doorstep. He was taken in and gradually nursed back to health by his caring mother and reintroduced to the precious daughter he had so long forsaken.

His mother had named her Mary, after his late wife, and she soon became his reason for living; the center of his world.

Within two years, he had rejoined the ministry and been offered a church in the Cove. And now, he and his Mary were inseparable. They were a joy to all and adored by nearly everyone.

"I just wanted to thank you for managing the situation so well," he said. "And, you don't have to worry about her showing up at your doorstep unannounced any time soon. She's going to have plenty to keep her busy right here for some time to come."

"I'm sure she will," Ma said, "but in all truth, she was no trouble at all. She is truly a lovely girl."

"That's good of you to say," Then glancing off into the distance, he suddenly said, "I'm so sorry ladies, please excuse me. I see Brother Harold and I must speak with him before he gets away."

"Certainly, Brother Wilson," Ma said. "And it was a lovely service."

With that, he once more shook hands with Pa, Forrest, and Diver, and hurried off to intercept Brother Harold.

When he was gone, Sarah May turned to Ma and asked, "What was that all about?"

Ma got a big smile on her face and began, "Well, the day of the big storm. . ."

She told Sarah May how Mary had shown up to visit, out of the blue, and agreed to go apple huntin' in Diver's place. She told her about the sight of me ridin' off on Joleen, the big mule, as Mary followed on Fancy, her little pony. And how we had returned looking like drowned muskrats. She finished off with the *hand-me-downs* and how Diver had delivered Mary home to the pastor wrapped up in an old tarp like a piece of fine furniture.

Sarah May was delighted.

"You slay me," she laughed as she grasped Ma's hands. "I think I'd rather listen to your stories then go to one of them highfalutin plays I've heard tell about in New York or Philadelphia."

"Well, just come live on a mountain with three men and you'll wind up with all the fixin's for story tellin' that you can handle." said Ma.

Diver was unusually quiet on the way home that day. Ma and Pa had long ago accepted his occasional spells of introspection. They would talk among their selves, occasionally drawing me into the conversation.

By the time we got home, Diver had reached a decision and said, "Zeb, I got something to discuss with ya."

"Sure," Pa said, "let's go in and have a cup of coffee. We'll talk at the table."

After heatin' up the coffee left over from breakfast, and adding generous servings of sugar and fresh cream, they got down to business.

"Way I see it," said Diver. "We stand to have a bumper crop of corn."

Pa nodded, "Sounds fair," he said.

"I figure from the looks of those ears, that virgin soil infused with years of natural mulch, very well may yield thirty-five, maybe forty bushels to the acre."

"That's unheard of," said Pa, an astounded look on his face.

"That may be," said Diver, "but an untouched mountain field like that one is unheard of too."

Pa pondered that a while and then said, "Do you have any idea what that would be worth?"

"Actually, I do," said Diver. "We have about forty acres, and if it yields forty bushels an acre, that's sixteen hundred bushels."

Pa nearly dropped his coffee cup.

"According to the posted price at the Abrams Creek Mill, corn is going for forty cents a bushel. That times sixteen-hundred bushels equals six hundred and forty dollars; before milling costs and freight."

"And, at prime?" Pa said.

Diver sipped his coffee and said, "Well now, that's what I wanted to talk to you about."

He looked Pa in the eye and said, "I was thinking. There's a lot of people gonna be hurtin' this winter after losin' their crops in that flood."

"Yeah?" Pa said, looking a bit nervous.

"Well, it seems to me that we never expected to get prime anyway. So, by keeping our crop right here in the Cove at regular market prices, we could help a lot of folks. Once the Cove is taken care of, the rest could be exported at a premium."

"We don't have a big enough crop to feed the Cove," Pa said.

"That's true," said Diver, "but if we got the other farmers whose crops weren't destroyed to join us," he threw up his hands in a questioning gesture as he added, "who knows? We could consolidate our crops and sell as a whole."

Pa thought about that for a moment. "Even if we could pull it off, how would those who need the corn, afford it? They took quite a beatin'."

"We give it to 'em on credit. Two years, no interest. We can also talk to any farmers who hire temporary help throughout the year to see if some of the cost could be worked off."

Pa sat there staring into his coffee cup for a while. He then looked up at Diver and said, "If not for you, we wouldn't have that cornfield. It was your vision, your drive, and your irrigation system, which made it possible. As far as I'm concerned that field is more yours than mine. If you want to try this thing, I'm all for it. But convincing the others? Well, that may be a tall order."

Diver nodded. "I'll go talk to Orwell. He could be a pivotal factor in this whole thing. If he's game, I'll have him spread the word and we'll have a meeting of the farmers at the Cade's Cove Baptist Church next Saturday."

Orwell was more difficult to convince than Pa had been. He was a businessman and usually had his eye on the bottom line.

"I done lost about a third of my crop as it is. Now you want me to forego the premium price and sell on credit to boot?" said an astounded Orwell. "You must be mad."

Diver grinned at the label thinkin' Orwell may not be too far off the mark.

"Well, the way I see it," he said, "on the average year, you sell about fifty percent of your yield to the Cove itself."

"Sounds about right," said Orwell, not knowing where Diver was going.

"Then it seems to me," Diver continued, "that of all people, you would want to be sure those that's hurtin' don't up and move away. If that were to happen, who would you be selling your crops to next year?"

Orwell scratched his whiskered cheek and considered that for a moment.

"I reckon there'd be someone else come along," he said.

"Oh, I have no doubt," said Diver. "Three, four years, you'd never know the flood ever happened. But that sure seems like a long time a haulin' your crops outta the Cove, hopin' to find a market elsewhere, seein's how we could have prevented folks from leavin' in the first place."

Orwell considered that for a bit. It did make sense to protect his most reliable consumer base. Even though his brother Jud owned the local freight line, haulin' that grain any distance wasn't a cheap operation: not to speak of the risks of loss due to accidents and inclement weather.

"Okay," he said as he placed both hands in his pockets and looked Diver in the eye, "if you can convince enough farmers to go along with this to make it doable, you can count me in. I'll put out the word that there's going to be a farmer's meeting at the Baptist Church next Saturday."

"Thank you, Orwell," Diver said. "Your doin' the right thing."

"Don't thank me yet," he said. "It's up to you and Zeb to convince the others to go along with it. You came up with this crazy scheme, now you get out there and sell it."

Things moved quickly after that. All day Thursday was taken up with the whole family delivering that other cookstove to Long Star. It was Ma's first visit to Black Gum Shoals, and she claimed it to be about the prettiest spot she ever did see.

Long Star was thrilled and astonished with her new stove, and Henry was struttin' around like the cock o' the roost.

Now that Ma knew the way, Long Star said, "Don't be a stranger."

Ma laughed and said, "Knowing the way, and havin' the nerve to make the trek on my own are two different things. But anytime I can talk Zeb into bringin' me, I'd be thrilled to come."

On Saturday, the meeting was held at noon. Though the whole thing was Diver's idea, he wanted Pa to present it to his neighbors. He said it would be received better from a long-time founder of the community, than from a newly arrived outsider.

Personally, I think Diver was still tryin' to pay Pa back by giving him the credit.

". . . and so, that's the nuts and bolts of it," Pa said as he concluded his proposition.

Percy Blyth spoke up. "I appreciate what you're trying to do, Zeb," he said. "I truly do. But you gotta understand. I been strugglin' for six years; ever since I came to the Cove, to make ends meet. This premium on grain is my ticket. Sure, I feel sorry for those who hit a bad spell, but I gotta look after my own family."

"I understand, Percy," Pa said. "I'm not here tryin' to push anybody into anything. Each man here should follow his own conscience. Only you know your own situation. It ain't for me to judge ya."

Placing his hands on Orwell's and Diver's shoulders, he continued, "We're just givin' those who can, the opportunity to help their neighbors."

With that, farmers discussed between themselves the merits of the plan, and the potential loss of the premium price. On the other hand, consolidating their crops with Orwell's guaranteed one hundred percent sales, and perhaps they could continue the co-op in years to come.

By the time it was all said and done, about thirty-five percent of the gathered farmers had signed up. More than enough to meet the community's needs through the winter.

"Good job," Orwell said, shaking Pa's hand. "I never thought you'd pull it off."

"I don't think the right person is gettin' the credit," said Pa, as he watched Diver mingling with the new members of the first Farmer's Association in the Cove.

"Well, he may be the inspiration, but it was your speech that sealed the deal," said Orwell.

That year, not a single family was lost to the Cove due to a food shortage

THIRTEEN

The Preacher & The Teacher

TIME PASSED, AS TIME WILL, and the hearty mountain folks continued their struggled to recover. They were familiar with adversity and knew that with God's help, they would find a way through it.

In mid-August, Pastor Wilson had his big baptizing in Abrams Creek. Both churches in the Cove were involved, and it was a major success. People came from miles around. There were folks from as far away as Sevierville, and even one family that lived down on the Tuckasegee River in North Carolina.

Me and Pa both got baptized along with about two dozen other folks, and Ma was just as thrilled as she could be. Oddly enough, Diver, though he still could not remember who he was, could remember that he had already been baptized—just not where or when.

Early September brought the corn harvest. Diver had well pegged our yield; it was thirty-eight bushels to the acre. Orwell was flabbergasted, as no one in the Cove had ever reached even thirty-five.

By October many of the higher peaks in the mountains were already snow-covered. The Old Farmer's Almanac was calling for a harsh winter with an abundance of frigid, snowy days.

The new school year began on September second. Though Ma had been afraid our little rooster incident had driven Miss Melloncamp off; as it turned out her older brother who was a councilman in Knoxville, had secured her a teaching position in the big city.

Our new schoolmarm was a petite, twenty-year-old named Miss Shelly. She was about as pretty and charming as a body could be, and truth be told all the boys were downright smitten. Even Tyrone was too slack-jawed and mesmerized to cause trouble for the first week or so of school.

As for me, I was in a conundrum. I just couldn't seem to be able to take my eyes off Miss Shelly, and yet I could feel Mary's ire rising because I wasn't paying enough attention to her. What could ya do? Young love was tough.

Rolf told Pa he finally closed the gate on the canyon hog-trap in the early hours of the sixth of

September and had trapped nearly forty pigs. Since the canyon had its own water source, over the next several weeks or so it would simply be a matter of feeding them until cooler, 'butchering weather,' drove the prices up.

Reports began drifting into the Cove about dead or missing livestock, but not enough to cause alarm. Losing a sheep or a cow on occasion was simply the price one paid for living in the mountains. Most farmers spent a night or two vigilantly watching over their animals only to find the threat had left the area and they never had a problem again. But as October waned, and my birthday came and went, the losses mounted. Rumors began to spread that the killer bear was back.

A delegation was formed to talk to Pa about trackin' it down. They arrived by carriage and drew up into the front yard where Pa awaited them, having heard the ironclad wheels and newly shod horses' hooves clattering up the rise. Out climbed Pastor Wilson, Thom Grear, Abner Coleridge, and Mike Holdner.

"Hello, Zeb," Pastor Wilson said as he shook Pa's hand.

"Pastor," Pa said.

"We've been asked to come speak to you about this new bear problem."

"What bear problem is that?" asked Pa.

Pastor Wilson was a bit taken aback by that response, and said, "The bear that's been killin' livestock around the Cove."

"Yeah I been hearin' about the killin's," Pa said, "but I've not heard anyone confirm it was a bear. Could be wolves, coyotes, or even a cat."

Pastor Wilson nodded and shifted his suspenders which had ridden up some in the back during the ride from the Cove.

"Yeah I reckon you're right," he said. "Could have been about anything. But if it is a bear, or anything else for that matter, would you be willing to go after it? And if so, what would it cost?"

"Well it seems to me; folks are thinkin' it's the same bear I went after last year. And it could be. I made no secret that I wasn't sure if it was dead or not."

"No sir, you didn't," Pastor Wilson said. "It was a matter of finishing off the bear or saving Diver, and you chose Diver. I can testify to you sayin' that."

"Well I see it like this," said Pa. "If it is a bear and it's the same bear, I done been paid to kill it; wouldn't be right to take money twice for the same job. And if it's something else and I kill it, I'll get paid for the hide like I always do. So yes, I'll go after it, and I don't need a bounty to do it. What I do need, is if someone's stock gets taken, I need to know about it right away, not days later."

"Okay," said Pastor Wilson, "we'll pass the word around. If anyone loses stock or even just sees this predator, they're to report directly to you."

"Fair enough," Pa said, as the delegation climbed back into their carriage. "I'll see you in church Sunday, Pastor."

As the carriage pulled away, Pa wondered why it took four men to ask for his help. Why, three of 'em hadn't even spoken. It didn't occur to him that a year ago he'd have just as likely thrown them off his property as not. A man under the right influences, can make some mighty big changes in a year, but folks tend to have a long, long memory.

As it turned out Pa didn't need some outlying farmer to send word about the culprit. The creature's biggest kill was nearly in Pa's own backyard.

A few days after the delegation's visit Pa was working on his new, larger, tanning shed. He had built it a bit farther downstream on a higher rise, but still within easy access of the much-needed stream. It had a sturdy foundation, strong walls, and was in the process of receiving its last bundle of shake shingles, when Pa heard yells coming from the Cove trail.

Stretching up to look over the peak of the shed, he saw Pat running into the yard.

"Over here, Pat," he called.

Pat stooped over and put his hands on his knees while he panted and gasped for air. Then he looked around to see where the shout had come from.

Pa could understand the young man's fatigue. It was a long way up that hill from the Tudwell place, and it appeared as if Pat had run the whole way.

"Over here," he repeated, waving his arm.

Pat finally caught sight of him, gave a small wave, and headed his way. By the time Pa had secured the loose shingles on the roof so they wouldn't slide off, and had climbed down the ladder, Pat arrived.

"What's the problem?" Pa asked.

"The bear," Pat gasped. "The bear got the pigs."

Pa put a hand on Pat's left shoulder. "Calm down," he said. "Catch your breath and then tell me what happened."

Pat once again stooped over as he took several deep breaths.

Finally, he straightened up and said, "This mornin' Rolf went to feed the hogs y'all have penned down in that canyon. He said the place looks like a slaughterhouse. He counted six dead pigs scattered across the gully and the rest were crowded back into a crevice with all the big boars facing out and gnashing their tusks."

"Yeah they'll do that," said Pa. "Ain't nothing in the mountains that'll face down a passel of boars once they're in a defensive position."

"Anyway, Rolf hurried home and told me to come get you right away," Pat said. "Said you'd want to see the damage right off."

"You did the right thing," said Pa. Then looking at Pat's heaving chest, he said, "Why didn't you come by horse?"

Pat gave Pa an embarrassed smile, and said, "Halfway up here, I was asking myself that same question. I guess in all the excitement, I just didn't think about it."

Pa slapped Pat on the back and laughed. "Well, next time I reckon you won't forget."

Pat could only grin as his head bobbed up and down in agreement.

FOURTEEN

Unfinished Business

IT DIDN'T TAKE LONG for Pa to determine it was a bear that had attacked the pigs. In fact, from the slash marks on the swine and the enormous prints left in the dirt, it was obviously the same bear he had chased last year. Once Pa saw a print, he wasn't likely to forget it.

The good news was that bear hadn't gotten away unscathed.

You see, when a passel o' wild hogs is under duress it's common for the sows to herd away the young'uns while the big boars turn to fight. And from the looks of things, the big old boars must have put up quite a fight. There were tuffs of bloody, black hair scattered all over that enclosure. Them hogs may've lost some of their own; but doubtless, they did some damage. How much damage was yet to be seen.

Rolf, standing at Pa's shoulder, said, "What do you think?"

"It was the killer bear alright," said Pa. "And by the looks of that bloody hair he was hurt. I'm gonna follow it for a bit and see if I can tell how bad."

"You want me to go with you?" asked Rolf.

"No," said Pa. "Why don't you spread the word that anyone who wants some pork can come take what they like. No reason letting it all go to waste."

Rolf nodded and hurried to spread the word.

Pa rested his prized Hawken rifle, which he had grabbed before trotting down the hill, in the crock of his left arm. Slowly tracking the bears scattered prints across the rock-strewn canyon enclosure, he found a bloody smear where the bear had slithered over the stone wall. From there, the trail led to a small, cold stream where the bear had wallowed in the mud, likely trying to relieve the numerous slash wounds he had received in the battle. Then it headed toward the vastly unpopulated stretches of the upper mountains.

After a couple of hours, the trail diminished as a northerly wind scattered the fall detritus leaving only faint clues of the bear's passing.

Pa knew that with the shortening of the days, darkness would overtake him long before he could catch up with the bear and come morning the trail would be almost gone. He also knew from the way it occasionally dragged its left rear leg, and from the way it tore apart several small trees and bushes in its path rather than going around them, it was hurting something fierce.

A hurt bear tended to head for its home territory. The place it knows best and feels most secure. And as it so happened, Pa knew where this bear's home territory was. And he also knew the one place in that vast open wilderness that a person could intercept it on its way. The tunnel through the laurel hell.

Retracing his steps, Pa returned to the pig-trap canyon. Several people had gathered in the gloaming and pulled the pigs from the enclosure. They were busy loading them onto a variety of field wagons.

Pa waved as he passed without talking. He had a killer bear to stop.

Reaching the top of the hill in much better shape than Pat had, Pa relayed to Ma all that had happened: the slaughtered hogs, the tell tale signs of the fight in the pen, following the bear tracks and seeing the drag marks from the bear's damaged leg.

Finally, he told her he figured his best chance of catching up with the brut would be at the laurel hell that he tracked it to last year.

Before he was done Diver had come in and leaned against the wall listening.

"So, it's the same bear?" Ma asked.

Pa nodded as he began loading his possibles bag.

"Yeah, it's the same bear," he said. "I tracked the thing for the better part of two weeks last year. I'd not be likely to forget it."

"Yes, you did," said Ma. "And you were lucky to make it home." She glanced at Diver. "Both of you. Let someone else risk their neck this time. Why does it always hafta be you?"

Pa took Ma into his arms. "Come now, Kathryn, you know there's no one else. Every man has a purpose, a calling if you will. This just happens to be mine. This is what I do."

"I know," said Ma. "It's just that I sometimes get scared. I know it's silly, but I just do."

"There's nothing that you could do that's silly," said Pa, as he kissed her on the forehead and gently wiped the tears from her cheeks. "And I promise you right now. This will soon be over, and I will be comin' home to you."

Ma hid her face in his warm hunting shirt hugging him tight, and said, "Make it soon Zeb. Please, make it soon."

"So, when do we leave?" said Diver.

Pa looked at him. "I didn't know there was a 'we' to it," he said.

"Well I reckon you ain't looking to pack no hundred-pound hide on your back when you got mules to do it. And I also don't see you wantin' to be dealing with a team of cantankerous mules when you got a big ol' granddaddy black bear to kill. So, as I said, when do we leave?"

Pa considered what Diver said and it made sense.

"Okay," he said. "I figure it'll take that bear a good three days to make it to that laurel hell. Maybe more, dragging that foot the way he is. I'm planning on being there in two days. I can use your help, but it will be to stay with and protect the mules."

Diver nodded.

"And in case you forgot," Pa grinned, "the last time you were around that bear with a mule you took a dive off a waterfall."

Diver laughed, "I think you're the one who has forgotten...I did forget."

They both laughed at that.

Ma, on the other hand, just shook her head. Only men could find a scrape with death funny.

Pa took down his Pennsylvania rifle and kit and handed them to Diver.

"Take this," he said. "I'll use the Hawken. We leave first thing in the mornin'."

Ma said, "I'll have supper ready in about an hour. Then I'll make y'all some fresh corn dodgers to take along."

Pa smiled and said, "I sure do like your corn dodgers."

Sunup saw Pa and Diver well on their way. The long trek they had so laboriously endured with the travois the year before, was an easy two-day ride on the mules. The first night they spent in relative comfort wrapped in warm blankets as they sat around a generous fire and reheated some of Ma's delicious rabbit stew.

They immensely enjoyed the clear, cold, night air, the stars twinkling in the heavens above, and the companionship of two close friends. But Pa warned Diver that would be the end of the good life, at least until the ordeal was over. There would be no fire, no warm food, and nothing else that could warn the bear of their presence.

"I understand," said Diver. "How far ya reckon we hafta go?"

"Maybe mid-afternoon tomorrow we'll come to a small ravine nestled on top of a long ridgeline. It's blocked on the west end by a rockslide, but open on the east. In fact, on a clear day you can see that old Indian landmark called Pointing Rock from there.

"The ravine has plenty of forage for the mules and even a water source, though you may hafta break some ice to get to it. The entrance is plenty big to get the animals through but narrow enough to defend it if that brute should somehow get around me.

"I figure the rock walls should keep most of the wind off you, and if you stuff a cranny with grass, leaves, and whatnot, you should be able to squirrel away and do just fine."

"I take it that's where we part ways?" said Diver.

"Yeah, I'll have another three, maybe four miles to get to the laurel hell. That should put you and the mules well out of the fray."

"And how long should I wait if you don't return?" asked Diver.

Pa studied on it for a minute. "I'll be going on in tomorrow after you're set up. The bear, if he's coming, should be there the next day or the day after that. It could lay-up overnight if it made a kill. I'd say if I'm not back on the fourth day, come on in and get me."

Diver looked Pa in the eye. "If something goes wrong, that could be a long wait," he said.

"If something goes wrong with that bear it won't matter," replied Pa.

The next morning brought a ground cloaking snowfall. The first one of the year for that part of the Smokies. Not a breeze stirred, and in the calm, the big snowflakes softly drifted straight down transforming the world into a white wonderland. Even the very mountains seemed to hold their breath not wanting to disturb the solitude. Stillness reigned. And as often happens during a calm, the frigid air lost its bite. It was a beautiful day.

Making good time, Pa and Diver arrived at the boxed-in ravine shortly after noon. Pa ate several corn dodgers and a healthy slice of elk jerky while Diver prepared for a stay of several days. Pa would take no food with him that might alert the bear. A small waterskin would be his only source of refreshment. Two or three days without food was no great sacrifice.

Bidding Diver farewell, Pa set his course for a rendezvous with the bear. This time he knew only one of them would be going home, so the nearer he grew to the laurel hell the more care he took. Such care in fact that the last quarter of a mile took him nearly two full hours to traverse.

Upon arrival he crawled to the top of an overgrown hillock and scanned the area below. The clearing between the heavy valley underbrush and the tunnel in the laurel hell showed no signs of the bear. Just as he was counting on, it had not yet arrived.

Pa carefully slithered down the hillock and around the blown-down tree where the bear had killed his rival the year before. Not a scrap of the dead bear remained—not even its skull.

He knew that a higher elevation would be preferable, as it would give him a vantage point from which to see the bear coming, but there was no suitable prominence nearby. There was only the hillock he had just come from, and it was too obscured by limbs and twigs from the blown-down tree to take a reliable shot from. So, Pa crawled into the laurel hell and selected a spot for his intended ambush.

He laid out his ground cover for protection from the frigid earth, then wrapped his blanket around himself, and pulled as much of the closest green vegetation over his prone form as possible. With his concealment as complete as he could make it, he settled in for a long wait.

Nighttime was not long in coming. A light frosty mist crept along the frozen ground and a bone numbing chill settled over the valley. The insulating snow of the previous day still clung to wax-like leaves and the brown stalks of long dead grass, but it did little to alleviate the cold.

Pa dared not sleep 'cause bears were as likely to be nocturnal as diurnal and a man who lets his guard down doesn't last long in the mountains.

It was a long, cold night.

Predawn brought a welcoming calmness to the world and the chill lifted. As the distant sky slowly lightened from a gun-blue gray to a soft orange then yellow blush, a gentle warmth settled over the valley. By sunup, it was downright pleasant. But then, as Pa knew it would, the warming sun brought a northern breeze. Cold air was sucked into the calm, and in less than an hour the forest was plunged back into a deep freeze. Another bone numbing day had begun.

Time passed slowly as Pa lay on the ground. He dared not move to relieve a growing ache that worked its way along his long muscles and seemed to settle in his very bones. He remembered how, as a younger man, he had spent many a day in a prone position waiting on game to appear. His hard, fit body had never given him the slightest hint of pain or even discomfort.

Guess I'm not so young anymore, he thought.

Another night and morning drifted by as Pa fortified his concentration by listening to the sounds of nature. He concentrated on and identified every tweet, chirp, and squeak he heard. Nearby a Golden-crowned Kinglet hopped along, pecking in the forest debris for insects on the underside of fallen leaves. Farther down the valley, two tree limbs squealed as they were rubbed together by sporadic bursts of wind.

Then an unidentified snap caught Pa's attention as he laid waiting and listening to his suddenly quiet surroundings. There in the frosty stillness he heard a huff.

He eased his rifle into shooting position and aimed in the general direction of the sound. Time passed . . . all was quiet. Then at the edge of the valley undergrowth, he saw a frosty cloud of condensation rise above a withered batch of huckleberry bush. He shifted his rifle barrel slightly to the right, centering on the bush and slowly eased back the hammer.

He heard another snap, then a slurping sound followed by a muted sneeze.

He set his rear trigger, and lightly rested his finger on the front trigger. The slightest pressure would drop the hammer and ignite the black powder sending the .54 caliber ball on its way. Pa waited . . . and waited.

A lesser man may've let the heavy barrel of his flintlock droop as he tired from the long wait, but Pa was not a lesser man. He held firm. All he needed was for the bear to advance three feet to expose its chest, and its heart.

However, as any general knows, *"No battle plan survives contact with the enemy."*

When the bear finally came into his line of sight—unbeknownst to Pa, and unseeable in the tall grasses of the clearing—the bear was dragging a long piece of cottonwood branch in its mouth, interlaced with carpenter ant burrows...a favorite snack.

Pa fired.

At over 500 ft lbs of energy, the lead ball should have devastated anything it came in contact with. It was a perfect shot, and Pa had caught the massive bruin completely off guard. However, by the slimmest of chances, the ball glanced off the cottonwood limb and smashed its way through the bear's ribcage piercing one lung but missing the heart by less than an inch.

Seeing the billowing smoke from the flintlock's powder burn, the bear charged in an instant. Pa had no time to reload. Dropping his weapon, he pulled his Bowie knife and dove into the sturdy limbs of the blown-down tree. A shattering crash of near earsplitting intensity followed in his wake. The entire tree shuddered and shifted from its longstanding resting place leaving deep furrows in the frozen ground. The pure mass and power required of any animal to shift such a weight was unimaginable.

Pa flipped over on his back and wiggled as best he could under some of the larger limbs as he thrust and slashed at the monstrous muzzle edging its way ever closer with each shake of its massive head.

Great bands of knotted muscle bunched and bulged under the thick, coal black coat of the enraged beast as it threw its massive weight against the few hardened branches that strained to withstand its frenzied on-slot.

Hot putrid breath and spittle billowed into Pa's face, and bloodshot, devil eyes bored into his soul. A thick cloud of condensation gathered among the twisted limbs as they snapped and popped, sounding like rapid gun shots in the frigid morning air. The ear-shattering bellow of the enraged bear, mere inches from Pa's face, was about more than a man could endure.

The bear popped its teeth and fought to bring its massive paws and sharp, black claws into play. It was only a matter of time before the behemoth ripped its way through the splintering cage-work of limbs and reached its prey.

Boom! A deafening report overshadowed the vicious snarling. The bear roared and pulled back just enough for Pa to see Two Hand charging through a cloud of drifting gun smoke. He tossed his rifle to the side and jumped onto the back of the ferocious beast. Hanging on with his legs wrapped around its waist and his left hand clamped onto one ear, he drew his Bowie knife and began thrusting it to the hilt.

The creature went crazy. It gnashed its jaws and whipped around its massive head, trying in vain to reach the antagonist on its back. It clawed the ground as it spun in circles and bellowed in rage.

While this was going on, Pa shimmied out from under the tree and rushed to his rifle. As he poured a charge down the barrel, the bear caught a claw in Two Hand's leather over-jacket and flung him across the clearing. He landed next to a sturdy log which shielded him from the worst of the beast's enraged retaliation against him.

Without taking the time to place a patch, Pa thumbed a ball into the barrel of the Hawken and slammed the butt plate onto the ground to seat it. By this time, the bear had Two Hand on his back and was flailing away with its deadly claws, even as Two Hand continued slashing with his Bowie knife.

As the battle continued, Pa ran up and placed his barrel directly on the back of the bear's neck. He knew it was a gamble to shoot the bruin while Two Hand was beneath it, but time was of the essence. He pulled the trigger sending a .54 caliber ball through the bears spine. With a huff, the monster collapsed on Two Hand's legs. Its huge jaws gave one last snap, rending nothing but its own tongue. The beast exhaled for the last time and died. The battle was over.

Pa dropped his rifle and leaped over the bear to reach Two Hand. The old shaman was unconscious and had a large piece of flesh hanging loose over his right ear. His shirt and jacket were in tatters. His exposed chest was torn and shredded with four long claw marks starting just below his left shoulder and continuing to his sternum. Two ribs could be seen through the bloody mess, and one of them was obviously broken.

As Pa continued his examination, he noted Two Hand's right shoulder blade had received a glancing bite, and his right forearm was broken. How he had continued to fight as long as he had, Pa couldn't fathom.

As gently as he could, Pa pulled Two Hand out from under the bear. He then cleaned the wounds with the water from his water skin and used strips of cloth cut from his blanket to wrap the wounds and staunch the heavy flow of blood. Slicing two pieces of flat wood from the log at Two Hands side, he used them to set his arm—tightly wrapping it with another section of his blanket.

In addition to the more serious upper body wounds, and the numerous scrapes and bruises, Pa found a badly shredded little toe sticking out of a hole in Two Hand's moccasins. Some wounds in battle can be downright mysterious.

FIFTHTEEN

Questions

DIVER CALLED OUT, "Hello, Zeb. are you there?"

Pa had just finished bandaging Two Hand when he heard Diver calling.

"Over here, Diver," he yelled. "Come on in."

Diver soon appeared, pulling the two nervous mules behide him. They could smell the bear and weren't too happy about it.

"I heard the shots and figured it was over one way or the other, so I loaded the mules and came on down," Diver said.

"Well, I'm glad you did," said Pa. As he talked, he moved to the side and Diver saw Two Hand for the first time.

"Who ya got there?" he asked, as he tied off the mules to the blown-down tree and hurried over to help.

"Its Two Hand, and he's hurt bad."

"What's he doing here?" asked Diver. "I thought we were alone"

"So, did I," said Pa. "He just kinda has a way of showin' up when you least expect him."

"I was here two days before you stumbled in," whispered Two Hand.

Pa and Diver were both startled by the voice and quickly kneeled by the old shaman's head. Diver snatched off his water skin and handed it to Pa, seeing his was empty.

"Just lay still, old man," Pa said, as he uncorked the skin. "You're hurt bad. You want some water?"

Having never opened his eyes, Two Hand let his lips part, and Pa dribbled cold water over his parched tongue. A slight shifting of his Adam's apple was the only indication that he had swallowed the life-giving liquid. Then he laid still.

"I think he's out," said Pa.

Diver had been lookin' back and forth between the massive bear and Two Hand. He pictured what had happened and marveled that the man still lived.

"What are we gonna to do with him?" he asked.

"I been thinking about that," said Pa. "I figure Long Star's place is the closest. It ain't but six or seven hours from here—though that is some mighty steep terrain. If I can get him there, Henry can fetch an Indian healer and Two Hand just might have a shot. He'll get a whole lot better treatment than that quack, Kendree, gave. After that, I reckon it's up to God."

Diver agreed it was a good plan.

"I'll unload the mules," Diver said. "We can wrap him up good in our blankets and tie him onto Joleen's pack saddle and you can ride old Mac. I'll wait here and skin the bear while you get him to Long Star."

"It's gonna get mighty cold out here without blankets," said Pa.

"I've still got a ground cover, and I'll build a good fire," said Diver. "Don't you worry about me. Two Hand needs them blankets a lot more than I do."

With that, they both got busy, and in short order they had Two Hand wrapped up and strapped on a pack saddle. Luckily, the old Indian remained unconscious, so he was spared the pain of being trussed up and shuffled around.

"Barring unforeseen problems, I should get there around midnight or by early morning. I'll need to give the mules a bit of a break, but I'll try to be back here by midday, or maybe a bit latter," said Pa.

"Not to worry," said Diver. "You just do what you need to do. I'll be fine."

Diver had no idea Pa was into his third day with any sleep—though it wouldn't have done any good if he had known it. Pa was fixin' to take Two Hand to Long Star.

Diver did know, Pa had been the best part of that time with no food. He firmly strapped the food pouch and a water skin to Mac's saddle.

Pa waved and disappeared into the thick brush of the long valley headed toward Pointing Rock. After reaching the prominence, he would be out of the valley and beyond the long canyon to the east. He could then cut across a half-dozen ridges or so, to reach Long Star's cabin.

After Pa left, Diver took his remaining water skin and found a clear spring to refill it. He then built a makeshift shelter in the branches of the blown-down tree and built a fire nearby. Finally, he got started on skinnin' the bear and carvin' out the more desired cuts of meat.

The bear was a good seven-and-a-half-feet long between pegs, tip-of-nose to tip-of-tail. And it must have weighed near half-a-ton. Perhaps not the biggest bruin that ever roamed the back mountains, but if not, he couldn't have been far from it.

Skinnin' it would have been much easier with the use of the mules, but Diver made do by skinnin' and butcherin', as he went.

A person would think a nine-hundred-plus-pound bear would give massive amounts of meat, but in reality, it was so old, only the choicest parts were worth keeping. The real prize was the mountain of late season fat the bear had built up that could be rendered down into oil.

By dark, Diver had finished his labors and drug most of the carcass well away from camp to help keep the scavengers at bay. The hide, he draped over his shelter as a rain repellent and hoped no other critters around were brave enough to check it out. The cuts of flesh and the mound of fat, he wrapped in a ground cover. It was far enough from the fire to keep from spoiling, yet close enough for him to protect.

With a roasted bear steak under his belt and a long slug of cold water quenching his thirst, Diver laid down on his remaining ground cover and prepared for bed. It was just after nine o'clock.

By ten o'clock he was wrapped up tight in the ground cover, sitting as close to the blazing fire as he could stand, and there he remained for the rest of the night.

A clear night, and full moon aided Pa in navigating through the nocturnal back country. It also dropped the temperatures well into the teens. Every hour or so he stopped to check on Two Hand, and to stomp around to get the blood moving in his limbs.

Then he climbed back on his mule and they continued on their journey. Many times, during that ride he thanked God for Diver, Clarence, and the mules. Without them, Two Hand would surely be a dead man.

It was a quarter 'til two in the mornin' when Pa rode up to the front of Long Star's cabin. The last hour or so had been pure torture and he wasn't sure if he could dismount without falling, so he hailed the house. The glow of a stoked fire could be seen filtering through small chinks between the timbers.

"Who is it?" called a voice from in the cabin.

"Zeb Banion," he responded.

He heard the wooden bar lift and then the door opened. Standing outlined in the weak light of the fireplace stood Henry, bow in hand. Pa sat monentarily startled. For a fleeting instant he thought he was looking at Jim. He hadn't noticed before, but the boy was growin' into his father's spittin' image.

"Zeb is that you?" said Long Star, as she looked out from behind her son and protector.

"It's me," he said. "I have Two Hand with me. He's hurt."

Long Star gasped and hurried past Henry.

"What happened?" she asked as she rushed to the mule carrying Two Hand.

"Bear," said Pa. "He's hurt bad."

Henry laid the bow aside, and said, "How about you, Mr. Banion? Are you okay?"

"Yeah, just half frozen," said Pa. "Help me down."

Henry reached out and steadied Pa as he climbed down from the mule. Then, after Pa regained his balance, they lowered Two Hand from Joleen, and carried him into the house.

"Place him on my bed," Long Star said.

She then immediately began unwrapping the dressings Pa had put on him and examining the wounds.

"E do da," she moaned in a weak voice.

E do da? . . . Father? Henry wasn't sure what he had heard but he didn't feel this was the time to ask.

Long Star suddenly grabbed Henry by the arm and looked him in the face. "Go to Uku Tsali. Tell him to bring the medicine woman, Ahyoka."

Then she squeezed his arm tight and looked him straight in the eye. "Tell him, Two Hand is injured. Say Long Star says, no one else is to know."

She let go of his arm, and said, "Now hurry."

Henry quickly dressed and raced out into the night.

Long Star looked at Pa. "What happened?"

Pa said, "He saved my life."

Long Star just nodded, then seeing the fatigue in Pa's face, she said, "You look done-in yourself. Lay on Henry's mat and get some sleep. Henry's got a half hour run ahead of him, and I don't expect them to get back for at least a couple of hours."

"But, Two Hand," Pa started to protest.

"I'll take care of him," she said. "There's nothing more you can do now. You need to rest."

Pa finally relented and laid on Henry's hide covered sleeping mat. He was out when his head hit the rolled straw pillow.

Diver was one happy man when the first rays of false dawn crept into the eastern skies. He pitched a couple more limbs onto his fire and rotated around for the thousandth time trying to thaw both his front-side and his back. He may have spent a longer night in his life, but if so, he sure couldn't remember when.

Strips of skewered bear meat dripping in hot fat, and corn dodgers thawed on a hot rock, helped revive his spirits.

Then, knowing he still had a long wait for Pa, and a need to keep movin', he began scrapin' the bear hide. It was hard but welcome work.

≈

Pa awoke when the door opened and Henry led Uku Tsali and Ahyoka inside. They immediately spotted Two Hand sprawled out on Long Star's bed and the old healer went to his side.

Pa arose and watched as Ahyoka carefully examined each of the wounds on Two Hand's ravaged body. No sooner had she looked over the visible cuts and contusions than her rough, withered hands began probing his aged flesh in search of any signs of unseen breaks or ruptures.

Long Star had already removed Two Hand's moccasins and when Ahyoka saw the shredded little toe, she simply pulled a small straight blade knife from a leather pouch and cut it off. She then pulled a half burned stick from the fireplace and blew on the reddened tip. Satisfied with the glowing ember, she carefully used it to cauterized the pulsing flow of blood. The resulting hiss of flesh and tendril of odorous smoke was ignored as she continued with her ministrations.

As Ahyoka worked, Long Star introduced Pa to Utu Tsali.

"It means Chief Charlie," she said.

Utu Tsali shook hands with Pa.

"And you, Zebulon Banion, I know," said Utu Tsali. "The Cherokee call you 'One Who Lives,' 'Friend of Two Hand and Jim Rainwater,' and 'He who pulls life from the water.'"

"I am honored," said Pa.

"It is said," said Utu Tsali, bringing the conversation to an end.

After a thorough examination, Ahyoka turned to Long Star and Pa.

"His spirit is strong," she said. "If he wishes to live and the Great Spirit agrees, he will live. You have done well, Zebulon Banion." And with that, she went on cleaning and suturing Two Hand's wounds.

Pa took Long Star's hands in his, and said, "I believe Ahyoka is right. He's as strong as they come, and he'll be around for a long, long time. I'm sure of it."

A single tear wet Long Star's cheek. "I pray you are right," she said.

"Now, I must go," Pa said. "I left Diver where the attack happened."

Long Star looked up at Pa with dark, damp eyes. "Thank you for bringing him here," she said. "May the Great One go with you. And Zeb, come back soon. You and Kate."

"I will," said Pa. Then he picked up the blood stained blankets that Two Hand had been wrapped in, and prepared to start on his journey.

Henry stood back out of the way contemplating all he had heard. *Had Ma really called Two Hand Father?* It make no sense. *And why can't anyone else know Two Hand is injured? And why does Utu Tsali hold Mr. Banion in such a place of honor?*

Youth is wrought with many questions only long seasons of life can answer.

SIXTEEN

Clive

BY THE LOOKS OF THE MUTED SUN, Diver figured it was near noon when he first became aware of the sound of shuffling leaves and snapping twigs as Pa's mules pushed their way through the frozen thickets of the valley.

The region was overcast, and the gossamer-like wisps of low-hanging clouds entrapped both sound and heat, making it a quite pleasant morning. A much welcome relief after the bone-chilling frost of the previous night.

"Hello, the camp," came Pa's age-old call.

"Come on in," replied Diver, who paused in his task of hide cleaning, and retrieved a couple o' strips of bear meat from his ground-cover-wrapped stash, knowing Pa would be famished after his long ride.

As Pa entered camp, Diver had just placed the skewered meat across 'Y' shaped sticks near the fire and scattered frozen corn dodgers on a hot stone.

"Have some lunch for you, in just a bit," he said.

"Much obliged," said Pa, as he climbed down from Mac's back. He then pulled the saddles and blankets off the mules and placed them on a handy limb before grabbin' a handful of brown grass to wipe Mac down with.

When the meal was ready, Pa told Diver about the trip to Long Star's cabin, his meetin' Chief Charlie and the medicine woman, and her prognosis of Two Hand's condition.

"And what do you think?" asked Diver. "Do you think he'll make it?"

Pa thought for a moment. "Yes, I truly think he will," Pa said.

If anyone knew the strength and determination of the old shaman, it was Pa.

"And how was your night?" Pa asked, knowing Diver had been left with little in the way of comforts.

"Fine, fine," he said. "Had to warm my back-side a time or two, but nothin' to talk about."

Pa nodded to Diver and grinned to himself, as he ate his last heated corn dodger. You couldn't get that man to complain if you filled his sleepin' mat with rattlesnakes.

When Pa was finished, they loaded up the mules and set out for home. The mules didn't at all take kindly to havin' a bear hide and meat on their backs, but soon settled down; and with Pa and Diver leading them they made good time.

By early evening of the third day, they finally made it home.

"Ma, they're here," I shouted as I saw them round that small corps of hemlocks in the meadow. Ma came rushing from the house, and we waited on the front porch as they approached.

Diver, being Diver, waved to us and then took Pa's lead rope.

"I'll take care of the animals," he said.

Pa nodded his thanks and hurried over to where me and Ma waited. To my astonishment, he took Ma into his big arms and kissed her—right there on the porch in front of God and everybody. I reckon if Pa hadn't been holding her up, Ma's knees would o' gave out and she'd a slumped down right there on the floor.

"I'm back," he said. "And I'll never be away from you that long again."

The bear hunt had taken eight long days.

≈

Supper that night was an odd mixture of joy over Pa and Diver being home, and somber concern about Two Hand's health.

Pa told us all about the battle with the bear, and Two Hand's unexpected appearance to save his life.

I could see Ma cringe with fear durin' the tellin' and I reckon she got about as white as a person could get.

Then Diver described the massive size of the bear and how it was almost beyond the capabilities of a single man to skin it. He said butcherin' it as he went was the only way to relieve the giant bruin of his hide.

When Diver finished his bear story, Pa told us 'bout takin' Two Hand to Long Star's and how he'd met Chief Charlie and the medicine woman, Ahyoka.

"If any living man can pull through what Two Hand endured, it's him," he said. "Let's bow our heads."

After a short prayer for Two Hand's recovery, Pa said he and Diver would take the bear hide into the Cove the next morning. They wanted to show the Cobbs that the killer of their son was dead.

"It won't bring Joey back," Pa said, "but hopefully it will help that poor couple rest easier."

"Not to mention all the other folks that's been a fearin' that, that beast could show up at their doorstep at any time," Diver said. "I reckon it's about time this valley got back to normal livin'."

Ma had tears in her eyes thinkin' 'bout Joey Cobb and how his loss must torment his parents.

"You're a good man Zebulon," was all she said.

≈

People streamed from their homes to see the passing of the gigantic bear hide stretched out in Pa's wagon. Young boys took it upon themselves to rush from house to house, heralding the approach of the killer.

It was a joyous event for most. Pa and Diver were inundated with praise and congratulations. But as they neared the Cobb home, the scene became more muted and solemn. Everyone seemed to hold their breath wondering what the old couple's reaction would be.

When Pa pulled his wagon to a stop and set the brake, Diver alighted and entered the Cobb's dwelling. A large group of Cove residents had gathered to show support for the Cobb's. They waited in reverent silence around the wagon.

At least ten minutes passed before the front door of the house opened. Then with Diver's help, Abner slowly led his grief-stricken wife from their empty home to view the remains of their son's killer. It was shocking how much they had aged in only one year, but Pa took note that Abner walked from the house on his own two feet, and without a cane to boot. That was a testament to the curative care Diver had administered to him.

The Cobbs made their way to the back of the wagon and just stood there for a while holding each other as tears freely flowed down their cheeks. It was as if their whole reason for being had been stolen by this pile of hair and hide. The devil who'd been haunting their dreams was dead, but their loss lived on.

Abner looked up at Pa and placed a trembling hand on Diver's arm while he hugged his wife close with the other arm.

"Bless you, Zebulon Banion," he said. "And you too, Diver. I . . ." He searched for the right words, but they never came. Finally, he gave up, shook his head, and gently led his wife back to their empty house. A domicile of love . . . and devastating loss.

When they entered and closed the door, not a word had been spoken by the mass of onlookers.

"Let's go home," Pa said.

Diver nodded.

It was a more subdued trek heading home through the Cove. A cold mist had begun to gather driving many people back indoors, but Pa and Diver weren't the only ones still out and about. They passed and greeted the occasional wayfarer with a nod here, a tip of the hat there, or a two-fingered salute with the hand holding the reins.

Diver half dozed as he shivered in his warmest, but still inadequate coat, and took little notice of the passersby, whether riding or on foot. It had been a long, cold, painful ride. Diver always had carried a lot of empathy for his fellow man, and it pained him dearly to see someone hurting. Abner and Milly Cobb had endured their share, and he hoped seeing the bear's hide had given them some sence of comfort.

"It'll be good to get home," Pa mused.

Diver glanced his way and nodded in agreement just as a large, ugly, rust colored mule, missing half his left ear, and splattered in frozen mud, passed by. On the mule's broad, strong back rode a heavily bearded, portly man in a huge, mud-encrusted coat; and a skinny, young boy wrapped up tight in an old blanket that didn't appear to have been washed since the day it was woven.

"You ain't gonna get no argument out of me with no statement like that," Diver said, as anxious to get home as Pa was.

Pa smiled.

Diver started to settle back into daydreamin' when a sudden epiphany raked his conscience. He suddenly jumped straight-up in the wagon and looked back at the man on the muddy mule.

"Hold on, Zeb," he shouted.

Pa reined back on the team, and Diver nearly fell over the dashboard. Catching himself just in time to avoided a nasty spill, he regained his feet and called out to the stranger.

"Clive . . . Clive Wallis, is that you?"

As Pa looked back to see who Diver was calling to, the rust colored mule came to a stop and then turned sideways in the road. The bearded man held his open hand above his coal black eyes, as if shading them from sunlight.

"Homer?" he called. "Is that Homer McCoy his own self I'm a seein'?"

He gigged the mule into motion and soon had the ugly creature standing alongside Pa's wagon.

"Well I'll be," Clive said. "I been a lookin' for you for a coon's age. What happened to ya?"

"Well, we'll get into that soon enough," said Diver. "First, I want you to meet Zeb Banion."

As Pa reached across in front of Diver to shake Clive's hand, Diver said, "Zeb, meet my uncle, Clive Wallis."

"Your uncle?" exclaimed Pa. "And what's this about Homer McCoy?"

"That's my name," said Diver. "Craziest thing. As soon as I saw Clive, it all came back to me. My name is Homer McCoy, and this is my Uncle Clive. Well, he ain't my real uncle, but he's my aunt's brother, so that's what I call him. And I've got a wife named . . ."

Suddenly he turned to Clive.

"Charlotte!" he said. "How is Charlotte?"

"Other than bein' plumb sick from a worryin' 'bout you, she's hailin' fine," he said. "We 'bout give up on ya for sure, but not your little Charlotte. By doggy, she said to keep a lookin' for ya, and so that's what we done. Didn't reckon it'd matter much, but we couldn't face the hurt in her if we stopped. And now, here ya stand. She knowed the right of it all along."

Relief showed in Diver's face. Then he noticed a young boy of about eight years old peekin' around Clive's shoulder.

"And who ya got here?" Diver asked.

"Oh, this'n here's your cousin Dan's boy, Ran'l, or Ran, as most folks t'home calls him."

He reached back and tousled the boy's hair. "Seems he's been takin' some after his pa, and his ma asked me to take him for a spell and see if I can't rid the ornery from him." He smiled through his shaggy beard and said, "Oh, he's a good boy."

"Well what are you doin' here?" asked Diver.

"I'm a lookin' for you," said Clive.

"But what brought you here?"

"Well now, that's a bit of a tale," Clive said.

"Tell you what," Diver said. "You just fall in behind us, and we'll get in outta this cold with a hot cup of coffee."

"Ain't had no better offer all day," said Clive. He pulled his mule back so Pa could get his team under way.

"Come back just like that?" Pa asked, as the wagon wheels picked up momentum and continued sloshin' through the half-frozen mud puddles in the road.

"Just like that," Diver repeated.

SEVENTEEN

Diver's Story

WHEN THEY PULLED UP IN FRONT of the house, Pa said, "Y'all go ahead and put the mules in the barn. I'll have Kathryn put some fresh coffee on."

He climbed down from his seat in the wagon, and Diver slid over to take the reins.

"We're headin' over there to the barn," Diver said to Clive, as he pointed across the bridge.

Clive nodded, and Diver led the way.

When Pa entered the house, he called for Ma.

"She's in the out-kitchen," I called from my loft. I was curled up near the warm chimney, reading *The Prairie* by James Fenimore Cooper. Miss Shelly had lent it to me, and I could hardly put it down.

"She figured y'all wouldn't be long now, so she put on some coffee and is baking some fresh bread."

I sure liked all that fresh bread Ma made in her new bread oven.

"Come on down from there," Pa called. "You're gonna want to see this."

"Kathryn," Pa called again as he went out the back door.

I quickly closed my book and climbed down from the loft.

I reckon Ma heard him, 'cause by the time I got down into what we now called the dining room, they were coming back in the door. Ma had the full coffee pot in her hand.

". . . got company," Pa was saying, "and you'll never guess who it is."

"Of course, I'll never guess," said Ma. "I ain't expectin' no one."

"Well, hold on to your corset," Pa said, as if Ma ever wore such a contraption, "'cause we're gettin' visited by Diver's kin."

"Diver's kin?" Ma gasped.

"Diver's kin." Pa repeated.

"But how?"

"Just hold on," Pa said. "They'll be in here directly to tell ya."

Ma poured Pa and herself a mug of coffee, and I fetched myself a glass of sassafras tea, and we all sat at the table waiting.

Ma, as inquisitive as ever, started to ask Pa something, but he just cut her off with a raised hand.

"Patience, Kathryn," he said. "We'll all know soon enough."

I don't reckon it was soon enough for Ma; but finally, Diver and his kin came through the door.

"There you are," Pa said as he indicated the bench across from him and Ma.

"Have a seat." He then reached back and grabbed two more mugs off the counter and passed them to Diver, who was already reachin' for the big coffee pot.

Ma saw the thin, dirt stained boy who followed the black bearded man into the kitchen, and stood up to get him a glass of sassafras tea.

"Would you care for some tea?" she asked the boy.

"Reckon I would," he said, rather enthusiastically.

Pa laughed, and Diver grinned. The bearded man didn't take any notice.

"This here is my Aunt Becca's stepbrother, Clive Wallis," Diver told Ma and me, as he motioned toward the heavy-set man standing next to him. "And the young'un there is Ran. He's my cousin Dan's boy."

Looking at Clive, he said, "And this is Kate, Zeb's wife, and his boy, Billy."

"Mighty fine to meet ya," Clive said pickin' at something that may've once been alive in his shaggy beard.

"Homer here's been tellin' us 'bout the sitiation ya pulled him out of," the man said to Pa. He then sluffed off his long, heavy, woolen coat and tried to shake the road muck from it.

After several wet clumps of Tennessee mud had splattered across Ma's clean floor, he gave up and let the filthy coat fall right where he stood. Then he stepped over it and took a seat.

He then pulled off his slouch hat, reached back and slapped it on his coat a few times, knocking off some of its clinging dirt and dust, before puttin' it back on his copious mass of greasy hair.

"And how y'all been downright neighborly an all," he continued.

The man reached across the table with an open hand. "I'm a thankin' ya kindly. We'uns think mighty highly o' the preacher here."

Pa reached out and shook the filthy hand as he turned his head to look at Diver.

"'The preacher,' is it?" asked Pa.

Diver nodded, "Reckon so. Quite a thing for a man to forget, ain't it?"

Everyone nodded, and chuckled as they sipped their drinks. I was sittin' there in wonder that Ma hadn't pitched the burly stranger out on his ear for messin' up her kitchen—Diver's kin or not.

"Charlotte is alright, you say?" Diver asked Clive.

Clive showed big, tobacco stained teeth through his wind-gnarled beard as he smiled and reassured Diver. "Charlotte's fine as rain. May've dumped a bit of paddin' since ya been missin', but nothin' a mess of her pawpaw hoecakes won't fix."

Ma looked confused. "Who's Charlotte?" she asked.

"Charlotte is my wife," said Diver.

"Oh, you have a wife," said Ma. "That's wonderful. Do you have any children?"

Diver suddenly froze, and Clive reached out and placed his rough hand on Diver's shoulder.

From the expressions on their faces, Ma knew she had touched a nerve.

"I'm sorry," she said. "Did I say something wrong?"

The men sat there with their heads hangin' for a time before Diver looked up at Ma and said, "No Kate, you didn't say anything wrong. It was just hard rememberin'. I reckon that's why God gave me this last year with y'all. He knew I needed time to heal. Time to learn I still have a purpose in this life.

"You know, I've heard y'all make little comments now and again 'bout how blessed you've been that God sent me your way. I just couldn't reason it out for myself. Would God really strike a man's memory so he might be of benefit to strangers? It made no sense to me, but I figured if it was God's will then so be it."

He looked around the table at our family and smiled.

"But now, I know," he said. "God didn't strike me down and send me here to bless y'all. I was the one being blessed all along. Why, it was you, Kate, and you, Zeb, and especially you, Billy. Y'all were exactly what I needed; I just didn't know it. Y'all will never know what you've done by bringin' a total stranger into your house, your lives, and even your family."

I reckon we were all about as flabbergasted as three people could get. Why, there weren't nothin' special 'bout us. Fact is, other than Pa being acclaimed for killin' that bear, I reckoned we was about the most unspecial people a body could meet.

"Well I don't know anything 'bout all that," said Pa. "But I do know you been mighty welcome and still are."

"What Zeb's saying," said Ma, "is that you are family."

"I appreciate that," said Diver. "I really do. And as for if I have children, I had a son."

He looked at me before continuing.

"He wasn't all that much older than Billy here, when I lost him."

"Oh, I'm so sorry," said Ma. "If you don't want to talk about it, we understand."

"No," said Diver. "I haven't talked about it in a long time. In fact, I couldn't even remember it. Now I think I really need to tell y'all everything. To let you see just what this last year has meant to me, and what a blessing this family has been to me."

"All right," Ma said, "you tell us whatever you wish to. But if it becomes too much, we'll understand."

"Thank you," said Diver.

He thought for a moment, then looked Ma in the eye. "It's hard to know where to begin, Kate, so I guess I'll just start at the beginning."

He smiled and began.

"I was just a young preacher with my first church when I laid eyes on Charlotte McCall. It weren't much of a church. Just an old barn, down near the Tug

River in Kentucky, that my Uncle Si let me clean out to hold services in.

"But there was this fella by the name of Walt McCall that thought it was just fine. Why, he brung his wife and nine children five miles every Sunday mornin' to hear me preach.

"A more devoted man, I've never met.

"Charlotte was his oldest, and I hadn't ever seen a prettier gal in all my born days. Oddly enough, she thought some highly of me too, and joked that changin' her name from McCall to McCoy would be downright economical on the alphabet.

"Barely a year after meetin', we got married.

"Now I always did have a hankerin' to have a large family, and Charlotte felt the same way. So, we started right off trying to have us a child. Turned out, things didn't go as we'd hoped. Two years passed and we were startin' to feel desperate. Nothin' was happenin'. We just couldn't understand what the problem was.

"Then one day Charlotte came to me all smiles and giggles. She was glowin' like a sunbeam. It had finally happened. Charlotte was with child.

"It was a hard pregnancy, but on a beautiful spring day, as life was awakening all along the Tug River Valley, sweet Charlotte gave birth to our wonderful son, Dennis McCoy.

"It was the happiest day of my life. But as often happens, our joy was soon tempered with sadness.

"Ya see, after the mid-wife came out and handed me a fine strong boy, she went back in to finish up with Charlotte. They was in there a mighty long time, and I was about to get worried; then the door opened."

"Pastor McCoy," she said. "Come on in and see your wife."

"When I entered that room, poor Charlotte looked about as weak as a person could be. I wanted her to sleep, but she insisted on holding her baby first. I gently laid our boy on her breast and you shoulda seen her beam. We were both just as proud as two people could be.

"After a few minutes, I noticed Charlotte had dozed off, so I quietly took our baby and left the room.

"The midwife saw me come out, and said we needed to talk. She said Charlotte had had a real hard time and things hadn't gone as good as they could have. For now it appeared she would be just fine, but it would be best if I brung in a doctor just to be safe.

"Now gettin' a doctor to come down there to that canebrake holler where we lived wasn't no easy feat, but somehow Charlotte's pa managed it.

"Doctor Stu Walburn was his name. He was a no-nonsense man of science, and told it as he saw it. He spent perfaps fifteen-or-twenty-minutes checkin' Charlotte out, then washed his hands and stowed his equipment."

"She'll live, but she'll bear no more children," he said. "Then held out his hand and said, "Five dollars oughta do it."

"Charlotte was cryin' as he left. From the time Doc Walburn stopped his carriage out front, 'til the time he rode away, couldn't have been a half-an-hour, but his news shattered our dreams.

"As hard as the news was to bear, we took heart, and gloried in our son. He was the joy of our lives.

"Through that entire summer we delighted in his antics. We were, I'm sure, like most first-time parents. We believed Dennis was a special little man who would reach heights that we couldn't even imagine. I guess you could say, we were smitten.

"Then winter came, and we noticed he began gasping on cold nights. He couldn't get enough air. I became frantic. We sought out advice from everyone in the county that had any kind of medical knowledge. But no one could help. No one gave us hope.

"Finally, I travelled to Lexington and spoke with Dr. Frank Drewberry, the most respected physician in the state. I described all Dennis's symptoms and how the cold and night made them worse. He said he knew of the affliction. It was a lung ailment that had no cure. It would worsen until Dennis's small body could no longer fight it off. At best, he might live to see his fifth birthday.

"I pleaded with him for hope. Any kinda hope."

He said, "The best you can do is keep him as warm as possible in the winter—but away from smoke. In the summer, the outdoor activity will strengthen his body–if it's not overdone. The stronger the boy is going into winter, the better his chances of makin' it through. But even then, you will only be prolonging his life perhaps an extra year or two—no more."

"I didn't care. If I could get extra time with my son, I would do anything I had to.

"As time passed, Dennis and I became nearly inseparable. I made a rock stove that heated his room in the winter without releasing smoke that would damage his lungs. In the summer we spent all the time I could spare frolicking in the outdoors.

"As he aged, he became infatuated with the woodland creatures near our home. Inquisitive beyond his years, he asked me questions I couldn't answer so I sought out books on animals. We learned everything we could about animals, forest creatures and domestic animals as well.

"Then as word spread about my Dennis' love of nature, members of my congregation brought us books on plants, trees, and insects.

"It was a true outpouring of love because my flock had a hard-enough time doin' for their own. How they managed to scrounge up books for young Dennis was beyond me.

"We traveled throughout the region studyin' all of God's creations.

"Each summer Dennis grew stronger, and each winter ravaged his body as if in retaliation for the advances we'd made.

"By the age of eleven, we were studyin' rocks and minerals, and where to find the healthiest soil to grow the best gardens.

"I had to go away for ten days to a ministry conference in the summer of his twelfth year. It had been the longest we'd ever been apart, and I was frantic to get home. When I got there, I found that Dennis had created a wonderland of the most spectacular flora in the area.

"Charlotte and I walked among the plant life and thrilled at the majesty of it all. It was beautiful. But Dennis had overlooked two things. He didn't have a large enough water source to maintain it. The different plants needed different amounts of water to survive. Some of the lowland plants were very needy, while those from higher elevations didn't tolerate wet feet so well.

"To solve these problems, we found a book on the Roman Empire. It described how they built their aqueducts, flume systems, and even sluice gates to control the amount of water to any given area.

"We planned, engineered, and worked until every plant received the nourishment it required. By the time we were done, that whole garden looked like it had sprouted up naturally. It became a destination for mountain folk from miles around.

"Those fleeting summers God gave Charlotte and me with our precious Dennis were the most wondrous times of our lives.

"Then in the early fall of his fifteenth winter, just as the days became cold and the nights frigid, a flu spread through our neck o' the woods. We did all we could to protect Dennis from it, but to no avail. He began coughing in the early morning hours of a frosty Wednesday. By noon on Thursday, his temperature had spiked, and his breathing had become a harsh wheezing that ripped apart my heart with every hard fought gasp. His weakened body just couldn't stand the strain. My boy didn't live to see the sunrise on Friday."

There wasn't a dry eye in the Banion house as Diver wiped his face with his sleeve and continued.

"As you can imagine, I was inconsolable. Not to say it was any easier for Charlotte, it certainly wasn't. But we grieved in different ways. She found comfort in her friends and family. She spent time with people who knew and loved Dennis and could reminisce with her about him.

"I couldn't. It was just too painful for me. In fact, just seeing the countryside we had so often roamed together was more than I could bear.

"To tell the truth, instead of letting God comfort me, I held everything inside. If not for Charlotte understanding my needs even better than I did, I believe I would have died.

"It was Charlotte who suggested I get away. She said I should go somewhere that I could heal. She thought it would do me good to be alone with God in the wilderness. To take the time I needed to reflect on the fifteen wonderful years we had shared with our son.

"At first, I refused, thinking it would be unfair to her. But in time, as I became more despondent, her suggestion appeared to be the only way.

"She kissed me and told me to go; to be healed. She will be waiting.

"Clive here," Diver said as he laid his hand on his uncle's shoulder, "loaned me a mule."

He looked at Clive and shook his head. "I'm sorry 'bout ol' Agnes. She was a fine companion afore that bear got her. I'll pay you back just as soon as I can."

"Ain't no call to be talkin' such a thing to me," said Clive. "We is kin. Ya done cut me deep to be a figurin' I'd be hankerin' for payback."

"I know Clive, and I'm real sorry. It's just not easy on a man feelin' like he's beholdin'."

"Well ya ain't, so I'll not hear more of it," said Clive, as he loudly slapped his grimy hand on Ma's table.

Diver grinned and nodded. "Good ol' Clive," he said under his breath.

"Anyway," he continued, "I hit the trail with nowhere in mind and just followed my feet. Day after day I drifted trying to forget, and night after night the dreams came, and I relived my loss all over again. By the time I made it down here into these hills I was 'bout done for this life. I was desperate for relief, for comfort, for the pain to stop.

"Then I remember hearing a waterfall along the trail in front of me. It sounded massive, strong, and deadly.

"I'm ashamed to say that for just a moment I contemplated that it could be the solution.

"I suppose it was all these thoughts rolling around in my head that caused me to be so distracted that I wasn't even aware that a bear was in the area.

"The last thing I remember is apologizing to God that I had let such a vile thought enter my head. And then I woke up all wrapped up tight by a warm fire and hurtin' somethin' fierce.

"Then here comes ol' Zeb poppin' up out of nowhere and askin' me who I was. I can remember that seeming like the most ordinary of questions, and yet for the life of me I couldn't fathom an answer. I realized I didn't know. And until I saw Clive today on that big, old, ugly mule of his, I still didn't know.

"And so that, my friends, is how I ended up divin' off them falls, as Zeb would put it, and ruinin' Zeb's bear hunt. I assure you it was not by choice."

EIGHTEEN

Farewell

FOR A LONG TIME AFTER THAT, silence reigned in our dining room. I suppose each of us was reflecting on all the events that had befell us over the past year and how Diver's story explained so much.

Ma finally broke the silence.

"I'm so sorry," she said. "A parent should never have to endure what you did. I once heard it said that *God will never give you more than you can deal with*, so I reckon your memory loss was to protect you. But I can tell you now, God also sent you to help heal us. Not just this family, but this whole community. You truly have been a blessing, Mr. McCoy."

Pa just sat there kinda noddin' his head in agreement, all solemn like, then looked over at Clive.

"So, what did you say brought you to the Cove?" he asked.

"Well now," Clive started, as he used a dirty, cracked fingernail to try and dislodge a morsel of this mornin's breakfast from between his teeth.

"We'uns, like I said, set a heap a stock in the Preacher here. So's there ain't a soul in the whole of the Tug River region don't know we're a searchin' for him." (He'd finally dug out whatever it was he'd been diggin' for in his teeth. He raised his index finger before his eyes and looked it over, then stuck it between his lips to suck it off.)

"Anyways, Skink and Walt Web—them's some brothers back home. They heared 'bout some work over near Knoxville way. Puttin' in a new road or somethin' like it, I'm a thinkin'." (He'd once again held up his finger lookin' it over as if wonderin' why its tip wasn't quite as filthy as the rest of 'em were. He finally shrugged, twisted it in his dirty shirt and then continued his story.)

"Well, their cousin Eddy Crouse was ramroddin' the job near Knoxville, so they up and hightailed it over yonder figurin' kin would hafta give 'em some work.

"Boy doggy, did they get a learnin'. The way I heared it, ol' Eddy told 'em he'd done worked too hard gettin' his own self a good payin' ramrod position to throw it all away on a couple a no-'count, lazy, Tug River swamp rats—kin or no.

"Now iffen ya knowed Skink and Walt ya wouldn't be a judgin' ol' Eddy too harsh-like. Them is some lazy boys, them Web brothers, I'm a tellin' ya."

We none of us had any idea what all this had to do with Clive comin' to the Cove, but we didn't interrupt, just sat there listenin'.

"Well Skink and Walt, not doin' any good with Eddy, decided to lay-up with some more o' the Crouse Clan figurin' ta snag a meal or two before headin' back home. And it was while they was there samplin' some a Tom Bob's pawpaw mash, that they first heared tell that old Aunt Gertrude was bled to death by some quack down Cades Cove way.

"Well, now any kinda man that's gonna call hisself a man can't stand back and let somethin' like that go unanswered.

"Them Crouse boys let it be knowed that they was comin' for that murderin' fraud."

Pa said, "Yeah, we know about Miss Gerdy's death by that quack, Doc Kendree. It was a real shame. Unfortunately, Kendree ran off before any justice could be done, and them Crouse boys never showed."

"That be how it is, ya say?" said Clive. "Them Crouse boys never did show up?"

"Nothing was seen of 'em," said Pa. "Kendree ran off as soon as he heard they was comin', and he didn't even take the time to clean out his cabin."

Clive looked at Diver and winked.

"Didn't even clean out his cabin, ya say?"

Ma looked at Pa and placed her hand over her throat.

I just sat there slack-jawed. This was all the sudden like becomin' a real ear tugger of a story.

"Anyway" Clive continued, "it was while Tom Bob was a tellin' Skink and Walt 'bout that trip to Cades Cove—you know, the one that never happened—that he got to jawin' 'bout a feller that had showed up in that neck o' the woods 'bout a year ago. It was said that he knowed 'bout everythin' a fella could be knowin'. Everthin' but who his own self was, that is. Seems he'd plumb forgot his own handle and even where he hailed from.

"Ya know, Skink and Walt ain't never been mistook as bein' what ya might call thinkin' folk, but even they thought that tale was a bit on the peculiar side.

"So, when they came back t' home, they dropped by my place and after indulgin' in a bit o' my moonshine, they tol' me the no-name-fella story.

"Now that story got me to thinkin'. They said that fella appeared up down there 'bout a year ago. That ain't all that long after the preacher went a missin'. And they said he 'bout knowed all they is to know. That sounds an awful lot like ol' Homer. Then they said he plumb forgot who he was or where he was from. Well now, that could 'splain why he didn't come home, 'cause he don't know where home was.

"So now I done got my dander up a wonderin' iffen that might be the preacher down yonder. I didn't want to be hitchin' up Charlotte's hopes just to have 'em be tattered. So, I packed up and me and Ran come on down this way to find out for our own selves. And that's what brung us here and how we found Homer."

"Lucky for Diver, or Homer, that them Web boys went to Knoxville lookin' for work," Pa said.

"You can still call me Diver," Diver said to Pa. "Tell you the truth, it just feels comfortable here in the Cove."

"Well Diver, or Homer, or anything else they may call ya, I want you to know you've always got a home here."

"I appreciate that," said Diver. He looked at Pa, then Ma, and finally at me. "I'll always think of you as family."

Ma had tears in her eyes and couldn't speak. She just stood there dabbin' her cheeks with her apron.

"When ya fixin' to be leaving?" asked Pa.

"Well I reckon, since harvest is over and there ain't that much goin' on, tomorrow will be as good a time as any. Besides, I'm anxious to see my Charlotte."

"Yeah," Pa said, "I can understand that."

He reached over and massaged his left arm which had been bothering him of late.

"Well I want you to take the team and wagon, and whatever goods could be of help to you. You more than deserve it."

"No, Zeb," Diver said. "I'm not needing anything."

Then on second thought he said, "Well, I could take you up on a mule, if you think you can spare him. I kinda lost track o' mine."

Pa smiled. "He's yours," he said. "Take ol' Mac. I only wish I could do more for you."

"You've done more than you know," Diver said.

Then turning to me, he said, "And you, Billy. I believe I'll miss you most of all. You've been like the son that was lost to me. I had a big ol' hollow hole in my heart and couldn't even remember why, but just seein' you bein' you . . . I don't know, it just kinda filled it in little by little every day. I couldn't be prouder of you if you were my Dennis himself. To tell the truth, I think you saved my life just as sure as your pa did when he pulled me from that pool, and I thank you for it."

I rushed over and hugged Diver.

"I don't want you to go," I said.

"I know," he said. "But we will meet again. I'm sure of it. And we'll keep in touch. God's got big plans for you and I want to know all about 'em."

By that time Ma had come rushin' over to Diver and joined in on the huggin'. Pa stood there smilin' and when they was done, he shook Diver's hand.

"I'm sure gonna miss you around here," he said.

Conversation continued well into the night, on that last full day that Diver was with us. Stories were told and memories shared. Diver told Clive about me and Henry being lost in the cave after escaping from the panther. Ran was spellbound by that tale and I had to go get the panther hide and the storyteller necklace to show everyone.

Then Clive and Diver laughingly told us about exploits they'd had back along the Tug River. It sounded to me like that was a mighty lively bunch up there in Kentucky.

Ma told Clive about how Diver had nursed ol' Abner back to health from that pig bite, and not to be outdone, Diver gave a full body performance with high steppin' leg movements and flailing arms actin' out how Pa had taken on that giant, killer black bear.

Pa downplayed the whole thing and said the way Diver was jumpin' around reminded him of Diver and the honeybees.

That brought on a whole new round of joshin' and teasin' and havin' a real good time.

Finally, it came time for me to be doin' my chores. Diver of course was lookin' to help, but Ma and Pa put a stop to that.

"You ain't workin' on your last day here," Pa said.

Clive told Ran to help me out and he jumped right to it. Seems he had a bit of hero-worship goin' on after that panther story and wanted to hear more about it. I was a bit embarrassed at first, but it didn't take long before I kinda got to likin' it.

I'm just glad Ma didn't see the way I was struttin' around tryin' to impress that boy.

'Bout the time me and Ran got my chores done, and Ma nearly had supper ready, she had Pa drag the washtub out. She poured a couple o' buckets of hot water into it and laid a bar of not-too-strong lye soap and a towel beside it.

She may not have said anything about Clive plopping his muddy coat down on her clean floor; (though Diver, at the first chance he got, kicked the coat into a corner and nonchalantly swept up the muck,) but she sure wasn't gonna let a bunch of unwashed men eat at her table.

Me and Ran got to the washtub first, but it wasn't lost on me that Pa and Diver made sure they got their turns also before Clive dipped his whole greasy head and filthy arms into the lukewarm water. By the time he was done washin' and dryin' that soapy grey water had darkened considerably, and I suspect Ma had to plumb throw that towel away.

We had a real good supper that night. When Clive was done, he let loose a belch that would o' put to shame that ear-splittin' thunderclap that shook the kitchen window the night o' the big storm. I'm not positive, but I think it may have had three syllables. Then, he thanked Ma kindly for the fine vittles.

Ma, kinda shell-shocked and startled, stood there for a moment afore she came to herself enough to say, "Why, thank you Clive."

I half expected Pa to get out his checker set and challenge Clive to a game. I don't know if he figured it to be a lost cause, or if even after bathing in our wash tub, he didn't want Clive handlin' his treasured gameboard. Whatever the reason, it didn't happen.

Diver said it was gonna be a long day tomorrow so him and Clive went to bed down in the barn.

Ran spent that night in the loft with me where he sat running his hand over that panther hide while asking question after question about the wild chase, and the long crawl and most of all, the two days me and Henry spent lost in the cave.

Truth be told, it didn't really take much pryin'. I kinda got a kick out of expandin' that story every time I got a chance to tell it.

NINETEEN

Hinny

DIVER, OR HOMER, I SUPPOSE, (he'll always be Diver to me,) left the next morning, right after eatin' one of Ma's big breakfasts. He, Clive, and young Ran packed up a load of vittles, some jugs of tea, and a couple pounds of honey which Ma had fixed up for 'em, and I don't reckon they were in need of a thing all the way to their Kentucky home.

Pa insisted that Diver take that big bearskin he had used to make the travois to drag Diver halfway across the mountains. So, I'm sure he had a mighty comfortable seat on the trek home.

I won't tell you 'bout all the hugs and kisses and whatnot that went on that morning before they rode off into the shimmering glow of a Smoky Mountain mist, 'cause to tell you the truth, I'm just a bit dewy-eyed sittin' here talkin' 'bout it.

What I will say is Diver was right. We met again and it was much sooner than we figured it would be. Aw, but as Ma would have said, "Hooey." I ain't gettin' into that. That's a whole 'nother story.

At the time, I was just mighty sad to see Diver go.

"Well it looks like there's gonna be a heap more chores around here," Pa said. We were sittin' in the dining room havin' a bowl of cornbread and buttermilk as a midday snack. "Reckon I'll take on most of what Diver was doin', but when I'm a huntin' and trappin' it'll fall on you, Billy."

"I can handle it, Pa," I said, though inside that's not how I felt at all.

More chores? I would've rather had my rear teeth pulled out than be handed more chores. But what can you say? They had to be done so there's nothing for it. I's just glad Pa was gonna do 'em when he was around.

"That's my boy," Pa said, as he roughed up my hair.

Then turnin' to Ma, Pa said, "Well I reckon if we're gonna be gettin' to church come Sunday, me and Billy better be gettin' into the Cove and findin' us another mule. Joleen ain't gonna be able to pull that wagon by herself."

"You think Clarence might have another one for sale?" asked Ma.

"No," said Pa. "He's sittin' about right on draft stock. I figure I'll check with Hec Rucker, the blacksmith. He sometimes has a mule or two for sale."

"Well, I'm wishin' you luck," Ma said. "I'd sure hate to miss church."

It was still early afternoon when me and Pa stopped Joleen out front of Hec's blacksmith shop. The skies had cleared up and the sun was shining, though there was still a bite in the air. I couldn't help but think of Diver and his kin and hoped the weather would hold and they would get home safe.

Hec stepped out of his shop in a great cloud of condensation, and as was his way, he eyed Joleen with an appraiser's gaze before acknowledging me and Pa.

"How do, Zeb?" he asked.

"Fair as I got a right to," replied Pa.

I hopped down from Joleen so Pa could climb off.

"What brings y'all down off your mountain?" Hec asked with a smile. "Needin' some shoein' done, or maybe some more fittin's for that castle I hear you're buildin' up yonder."

Pa laughed. "Castle is it now?"

"'Bout the way ya hear it down here. Say you did a real fine job."

"Well now, I'll not argue that point," said Pa, "but it weren't me. It was Billy here, Diver, Forrest, Clarence's boys, and several others. Charley Wrightman did the furniture, and you ain't never seen the likes. She's one fine artist."

"Yes, she is," said Hec. "And one fine woman too, you ask me."

I think me and Pa were both a little taken aback by that comment, but we neither one let on none. I reckon when you thought about it, a big woman like Charley may o' been just what Hec needed. He was a mighty big fella his own self.

He may o' been a few inches shorter than Pa or Forrest, but he was broader and bigger boned and probably had a good forty pounds on either of 'em.

And strong, woo doggies. That man was 'bout as strong as a man could be. I reckon he would o' gave ol' Hercules, in them Greek legends a run for his money. They say he never wrestled at Orwell's Fourth Celebrations 'cause it just wouldn't be fair. 'Sides who wants to see the same person win every time.

"Yeah I reckon she is," said Pa.

"So, what can I do you for?" Hec asked.

"Well," Pa said, "Diver went on home and took Mac with him, so I'm in need of another mule."

"Whatcha mean, Diver went home? I thought he lived with y'all."

"He did," said Pa. "But he had some kin come find him and he went back to his real home. That's why I'm needin' a mule."

"I'm sure sorry to hear that," said Hec. "I only spoke with him a time or two, but he seemed like a real fine fella."

"That he is," said Pa. "Now, about a mule?"

"Oh yeah," said Hec, "I got a mule for sale. Come on back and I'll show it to ya."

We followed Hec through his smoky blacksmith shop. How a person could work in that heat and smoke was beyond me.

Out back he had a corral bordered on one side by a small barn with a half dozen stalls. He had plenty of room for his own stock, and any horses left with him to be shoed.

Alongside the barn was two carriages and parts for various buggies and wagons. In the corral was two horses, three mules, a donkey, and a creature that I wasn't real sure about.

It was about the size of the donkey, but it had a head like a horse and a stout body like a mule. Its legs looked too thick for a horse or a mule. It had a full mane and a horse-like tail, but its ears were more like a donkey's; not as short like horses' but not as long as a mules'. It was an odd mix that I'd never seen before, but it wasn't a bad looking critter at that.

"Whatcha got here?" Pa asked, as he too saw the small equine.

"Why that's a hinny," said Hec.

"A hinny?" I said.

"Yeah a hinny," said Hec. "A mule is a cross between a male donkey and a female horse. A hinny is a cross between a male horse and a female donkey. That's why you see her over there with the donkey. A mule has a mare mother, so they feel at home with horses, but a hinny has a jenny mother, so they tend to stay with the donkeys."

I was a bit taken aback by all this new learnin'. Who'd've ever thought that if you crossed this'n with that'n you'd wind up with the other?

Kinda made me wonder what kinda crossin' it took to come up with a Clive.

"Where'd you come by her?" Pa asked.

"Well, they're pretty scarce, that's a fact," he said.

"A fella come through awhile back with a horse in need of shoein'. Said he was headed for Pittsburg or the like. Anyway, it was quite a ways and that horse o' his wouldn't've ever made it on them shoes he was a wearin'. The ol' boy didn't have any money, but he did have this here hinny. He offered the hinny for four new shoes and a poke of vittles that'd get him a few days up the road. I thought it was a good trade at the time, but now I'm a thinkin' I got hornswoggled. Ain't a soul in the Cove lookin' to be harnessed with a hinny."

"Can't be that hard to be shed of," said Pa.

"That's what I thought," said Hec. "But Jud Becket 'bout fixed my plow. Ya see he's a might upset with me 'cause I won't give him no special discounts for treatin' his freight stock. Figures just because he has a big outfit he aughta get a better deal. Well, I told him he'll pay like everybody else or he can find hisself another smith.

"Anyway, to get back at me he spread the word that hinnies may be as strong as mules, but they just won't work. They ain't good for nothin' but ridin', and who wants to ride a critter that nobody knows what it is?

"So, I decided to show him. I set up a trial workout for that hinny and invited folks to come and watch."

"So, what happened?" asked Pa.

"The stubborn critter refused to work," said Hec. "Couldn't do a thing with her."

Pa laughed. "Well now, the way I hear tell, you're a fair man and while you'd not try and put one over on a customer, you ain't knowed for losing out neither. I reckon you'll get by."

Hec smiled. "Suppose I can't complain at that," he said. "So anyway, there's the mules I got. See any you like; we'll work something out.

Pa strolled across the corral and looked over the mules. One was obviously not the most fit creature he'd ever seen, and it didn't take long to realize the poor thing suffered from gas colic. Ma certainly wouldn't have been pleased to ride behind a gassy mule all the way to and from church.

The other two both seemed in fine fettle. One was black and about as big as Mac, and looked to be as strong as a mule could be. The other, a grey, wasn't so large but also looked to be in fine health.

"Well what do you think?" asked Hec.

"I'm leanin' toward the grey," said Pa.

"The grey?" asked Hec. "I figured you'd go for the power-house. That big black is a mighty fine animal."

"I can see that" said Pa. "But the way I figure it, I need a team, and that grey should match ol' Joleen just fine."

Hec thought about that and said, "Reckon I see where you're comin' from. That grey *would* look mighty fine alongside your Joleen. And I don't see ya findin' a better match for pullin'."

"So, what's your price?" said Pa.

Hec studied for a minute and then said, "Ya know, you may have dropped by just at the right time. Did ya see them carriages I got back there by the barn?"

"I did," said Pa.

"Well look at this." He then took me and Pa into the back of his shop. On the wall, and scattered across a few benches, laid several sets of harnesses, reins, and stirrup straps. On sawhorses sat three saddles in varying stages of repair and hanging from a large hook on the wall was a finished pony saddle.

"Other than smithing, I also build buggies and do leather working. I can get all the cowhides I need right here in the Cove, but the heavy stuff for suspension work is gettin' scarce."

He handed Pa a piece of thick leather.

"Buffalo hide is two to three times as thick as cowhide. Take that little grey back there, and bring me two buffalo hides, with the option of dealing for more in the future, and we got a deal."

Pa nodded. He was used to barterin'.

"Tell ya what, throw in that hinny, this pony saddle and tack, and I'll add an elk hide to the mix."

"Well now, I don't know," started Hec.

"Seems to me, I'd be doin' you a favor takin' that no-good critter off your hands. And I promise not to say you hornswoggled me into it."

Hec laughed. "I reckon under them conditions, we got us a deal."

Pa rode Joleen home and led the grey while I rode the hinny. That pony saddle fit her fine and she may not have been a worker, but she had a real nice gait.

"What you lookin' to do with her?" I asked Pa.

"Well, I'll talk it over with your ma first. The way I see it, between Joleen and the grey we don't need any more ridin' stock, but your ma wants Long Star to visit more often and I figure that little hinny could help make that more possible. Anyway, I figure Long Star and Henry could put her to good use."

I thought that over. Way out there on their own in the wilderness, they could surely use a hinny to help get around. And seein's how Henry already had a goat to take care of, it wouldn't hurt none to throw in another critter. And since he always did seem to think it was mighty funny that I had so many chores to take care of while he ran free, I reckoned it might do him good to have a few more of his own.

"I think that's a real fine idea, Pa," I said. "I reckon they'd be plumb grateful."

When we got home and showed our newest acquisitions to Ma, she was plumb tickled. The grey she right off named Gabby 'cause it was constantly flippin' its lips and snortin'. And the hinny, she thought was darling. A perfect gift for Long Star.

TWENTY

Gone Visiting

P A HAD BEEN SPENDING a lot of time tannin' that big killer bearskin. Something of that size weren't no easy task. He'd finished the fleshing, salting, soaking, rinsing and brain tanning in about five days. Now it was time to work the hide as it dried to make it nice and soft. A smaller hide could be worked off and on for a day or so and have great results. He figured this massive bearskin would take four to six days.

A week and a half of hard work, but well worth it. After his Hawkins, that hide was his prize possession and he had big plans for it.

On Saturday, Pa rode the Hinny down to Clarence's place. He knew Clarence would get a kick out of seein' it.

"Whatcha got there?" Clarence said as Pa came ridin' up.

"They call it a hinny," said Pa.

Yeah, I heard of 'em," said Clarence, "But I ain't never seen one. Heard tell Hec Rucker got suckered into takin' one in trade."

"Yeah," said Pa, "this is the one Hec had. So now ya have seen one."

"Reckon so," said Clarence, as he looked the strange critter over. "Ain't that many hinnies around. Much less a jenny hinny. Whatcha fixin' to do with it? Gonna start a hinny breedin' farm?"

Pa smiled. It ain't easy to come up with a hinny to start with seein's how male horses and female donkeys don't have a natural attraction. And of course, hinnies can't bare young so it would be a mighty slow producing farm.

"No," he said. "I'm lookin' to give her to Long Star. I figure she could use a sure-footed ridin' animal out there where she lives."

"Sounds like a right neighborly idea," said Clarence.

"That's part o' why I'm here," said Pa. "I was fixin' to head out her way come Monday. I got some business to take care of and was hopin' to take Ma and Billy with me so's they could visit with Long Star and

243

Henry. Could be a couple days and with the crazy weather we have this time a year, who knows? I was hopin' one of your boys could see to our animals until we get back."

"Not a problem," said Clarence. "I'll have Pat feed and milk your stock. In fact, if it's okay with you I'll tell him to go ahead and stay in Diver's place until you get back. That way if somethin' comes up, you won't need to worry about the farm. Take all the time you need."

"That sounds mighty fine," said Pa. "Tell him to help himself to the pantry and springhouse. I don't reckon he'll starve none."

"You ain't never seen that boy eat. If ya take too long, we may have to restock ya."

Pa smiled and held out his hand. "Well I sure thank ya Clarence, and we'll try not to be too long. I hate takin' your help from ya."

"Don't mention it," said Clarence, shaking Pa's hand. "Ain't got that much going on this time o' year anyway. Let Kate and Billy have some time away. Do 'em good."

With that, Pa remounted the little hinny and turned her back toward home with his feet nearly dragging the ground.

Sunday was uneventful. A welcome blanket of warmth had settled over the valley sometime during the night and the morning temperatures were in the low forties on their way to sixty-five.

Most of the church congregation gathered around Ma and Pa asking questions about Diver's kin, how he had regained his memory, and what really brought him to the Smokies in the first place.

Everyone was sorry to see him leave but they all wished him the best in his re-found life, and they all hoped to see him again sometime in the future. Many told wonderful stories about him, laughs were shared, and heartfelt thanks were given.

During all this hubbub of questions and stories, it appeared to me that Pastor Wilson was oddly quiet. He stood off to the side; half-listening, and never did join in with the conversation. Somethin' seemed to be botherin' him.

"Hi, Billy."

I turned around and there stood Mary wearing her pretty, blue, Sunday dress. On her head was a blue bonnet sporting white piping and lacey ribbons which hung down and tied into a big bow beneath her chin.

Her clear blue eyes and long, straight, silky blond hair seemed to shimmer in the mid-winter sun and her brilliant smile was dazzling.

I don't know how she did it, but she always caught me unawares. I stood there and stared at her, not knowing what to say.

"You gonna say hi, Billy?" she asked.

That kinda woke me up a bit, and I said, "Oh, a, sorry. Yeah, hi, Mary. You're lookin' grea . . . I mean, how ya doin' Mary."

She just stood there, slightly holding her dress out to each side with both hands and kinda twistin' back and forth causing a little bellowing affect that was quite captivating. Do gals sit around and think these moves up?

"I was real sorry to hear Diver left," she said.

"Yeah, it was mighty sudden like," I said. "But at least he now remembers his family. I'd sure hate not knowing who I was, or who Ma and Pa were."

"Yes, that would be awful," she said. "Or not remember your girl?"

I was totally flabbergasted at that. I didn't know what to say. *My girl? Was she saying she was 'my girl'?* I suddenly developed a big ol' knot in my throat and 'bout thought I was gonna choke on it. Lookin' around, I tried to find somethin' else to talk about. Then I saw Pastor Wilson again. He had taken Pa over to the side, and just the two of 'em were havin' a quiet conversation.

"Is your Pa alright?" I asked Mary.

The question threw her off-stride. I reckon she was still in the flirtin' mood that I was trying to steer clear of.

"Well, he did get a letter the other day and he's not quite been hisself since."

"Oh," I said, "I was just wondering. He just looks like he has somethin' on his mind to me."

By this time, I noticed that the Pastor was headed our way and Pa was showin' Forrest his new grey.

"Hello, Billy," said Pastor Wilson as he walked up. Mary was no longer twisting around, but rather, she had her hands clasped behind her back as she smiled up at her father.

"Hello, Pastor," I said. "Nice day isn't it."

"Yes, it is," he said. Then turning to Mary, he said, "Time to go, Mary. I have a lot to do today."

"Yes, Pa," she said. Then giving a little wave she said, "Bye, Billy."

"Bye, Mary," I said.

Pastor Wilson turned to leave, and I saw Mary glance up at him to see that he wasn't lookin' before givin' me a wink. She then turned to follow him.

I'd just started walkin' over toward Pa and Forrest, and that little move made me stumble over my own two feet. Even with Mary's back to me, in my mind I could see a grin of satisfaction on her face. To tell the truth, I had to grin myself.

Monday morning was still uncommonly warm, but Pa said he didn't like the looks of the sky.

Here I'd hurried to get all my chores done, and now it looked like we might not be going anyway. Me and Ma stood on the front porch with Pa as he pointed out the leading edge of a thick cloudbank just starting to break the horizon.

"Then look over yonder," he said. "See them trees up on that ridge there? If ya watch their tops, you'll see 'em startin' to sway. It started on that ridge to the right, and it won't be long before all them hills full of trees are gonna be blowin' in the wind. When that happens, the temperature's gonna start to fall, and I reckon it's gonna get cold real quick."

"Whatcha sayin' Zeb?" Ma asked. "Ya don't reckon we should go?"

Pa continued to study the horizon. He looked like a man in conflict.

"Well, ya just don't know this time a year," he said. "That cloud bank could come in strong and dump a foot of snow on the mountains, or it could split and leave us without a flake. It's a gamble, whatever ya do."

Still considerin', he said, "Fact is if we wait, it could get better, or it could get worse. I'll leave it to you. If you want to hold off, that's fine with me. If you want to go, I'll get us there."

I knew at that point we were going. Ma never could wait if she had a choice. She was truly looking forward to seeing Long Star and giving her the hinny, and she knew I longed to see Henry. But mostly Ma knew Pa was concerned about Two Hand, and if not for us he'd not even give this weather a thought.

"Let's do it," said Ma.

Pa hugged her. "Let's do it," he said.

In no time, we were packed.

Pa was on Joleen, along with his Hawkins, possibles bag, and two burlap sacks of food stuff.

Ma rode a nervous Gabby who was draped in the huge bear hide, and I sat astride of the even gaited, as of yet unnamed hinny.

The first part of the journey we followed the trail that me and Mary had used when we went apple pickin' at the orchard. It was a bit out of the way, but Pa knew Ma would want to see it, and it was quicker than breaking a trail into the no-name-river valley were Pa made his pact with God.

Unfortunately, being mid-winter, the field of flowers was now a brown and yellow glade of dead weeds and the apple orchard was no more than a corps of barren trees.

But Ma, with her active imagination after years of listening to other people tell her of their journeys and adventures, could picture the scene in her head and was thrilled.

"It must have been beautiful, Billy," she said.

I just grinned and nodded, still not comfortable talkin' about such things with my Ma, especially in front of Pa.

"I'll bring you back next year," I said. "You can see it for yourself."

"That would be wonderful," she said, smiling and looking around. "Thank you, Billy."

I glanced over at Pa, and he nodded. I think he approved.

After passing through the orchard Pa pointed out the tree where the panther had been killed. Somethin' that I hadn't seen myself. Then, we climbed the steep slope the dogs had chased the cat down and followed a long mountain valley for a mile or so before reentering the hardwood forest proper.

The temperature had steadily dropped, and the winds had increased, as Pa foresaw; but the gathering clouds held their heavy burden, and we were spared having to travel in snow. All in all it wasn't bad, except for the few spots where we topped a ridge and had to face the full force of the biting winds before dropping down the other side.

Somehow, Pa led us to the narrow path that entered the south end of Black Gum Shoal and by a quarter 'til ten, we had arrived at Long Star's cabin. The journey had taken just under three hours.

As we stopped in the front yard, the cabin door opened, and Henry looked out.

"It's the Banions, Ma," he shouted. "And Billy's on a peculiar lookin' critter."

"Tell 'em to come in," we heard Long Star reply.

As if we couldn't hear her, Henry said, "She says for y'all to come on in," then he came out and looked the hinny over.

"Ain't never seen nothin' like that," he said.

"Yeah, they're pretty rare," I agreed.

"Y'all go on in," he told Ma and Pa. "Me and Billy will take care of the mules."

Pa jumped down off Joleen and propped his rifle against the cabin wall, then helped Ma off Gabby. He then loosened the straps holding the bear hide and draped it across his left shoulder.

"Now you can take the mules," he said.

Henry's eyes widened when he saw the immense bear hide. Two Hand had told him he had fought with a bear, but surely this couldn't be it. No one could survive an encounter with such a beast.

Only Henry's upbringing prevented him from questioning Pa about it right then and there. He knew if he was to know more, the time would come.

Taking Joleen's lead rope, Henry said, "this way." I followed him with Gabby and the hinny in tow.

As me and Henry led the animals away, Pa idly brushed the bearskin with his left hand and placed his right around Ma's shoulder as he looked at the cabin door. He seemed a bit hesitant to enter.

Ma reached up and squeezed his hand on her shoulder.

"He's a strong man," she said, understanding Pa's hesitance to see the great shaman weakened and vulnerable.

"I owe him my life," said Pa. "He's like a father to me."

"I know," said Ma, as she gently nudged Pa toward the door. "And no son could honor their father more than you have."

TWENTY-ONE

Black Gum Shoals

HENRY LED THE WAY to a small grassy clearing near a spring-fed brook.

"This oughta do it," he said.

The animals wasted no time sniffing out the more edible vegetation in the tangled mass of weeds and grasses and were soon happily munching away.

As they ate, I hobbled each one so when we needed them, they wouldn't have strayed far. We then pulled their saddles, blankets, and bridles, and stored them in a small log shed that stood nearby.

"That's one strange lookin' mule," Henry said looking at the hinny.

"Ain't a mule, it's a hinny," I said. "But you'll get to know all about that soon enough."

"What are you talkin' about?" he said.

"You'll see," I laughed. "But let's go inside, I'm freezin'."

When Ma and Pa entered the cabin, they were surprised to see Two Hand sitting in a chair at Long Star's dining table. He looked drained and his complexion was pale, but he had a half-eaten bowl of mashed-elk-marrow and squirrel-brains settin' in front of him, that he had been soppin' up with a piece of flatbread. Near his left hand sat a cup of spruce tea with flakes of ginseng root floating in it.

"Zebulon," he said, "and Kate. You honor an old man by coming."

"What are you doing up?" asked Pa. "Ahyoka seemed to think you were in a bad way. Wasn't even sure you'd make it."

"He should not be up," said Long Star. "Maybe you can get him to listen."

Two Hand waved his massive right arm in the air as if shrugging off Long Star's comment. He flung droplets of elk and squirrel across the table in the process.

"Women," he barked, before breaking down into a racking fit of coughing.

As the convulsions lessened, he wiped a trace of bloody spittle from the corner of his mouth and wiped it on his leggings. Pa watched as a rivulet of sweat ran down the old man's broad cheek and dripped off onto his long buckskin tunic.

After taking a deep, ragged breath, he continued. "Women, they think a man should lay around all day every time he's feelin' a bit low."

Long Star had her arms folded and was twisting the sleeves of her dress as she stood behind Two Hand. Concern was etched across her fatigued face.

"You're feelin' more than a bit low," said Pa. "You look like ya done a couple rounds with a half-ton bear."

Two Hand snickered, which brought on another round of coughs. He then shivered and said, "Reckon I am a bit tired at that."

As he began to rise his legs sagged, so Pa quickly threw an arm around him and helped him to bed.

"I might be a bit weaker than I thought," he said, as he trembled from another shiver. "Cold in here."

"I got something that'll warm you up," Pa said, as he reached over for the bearskin.

When he spread the giant hide over the shaman, Two Hand said, "Is this him?"

"It is," said Pa.

"He's yours," said the shaman.

Before Pa could answer, Two Hand was asleep with his hands clutched tight in the long, thick hair of the killer bear.

Pa accompanied Long Star and Ma back over to the table and they all sat down.

"Has Ahyoka been back?" he asked Long Star. "What does she say?"

Long Star bowed her head and nodded. When she looked up her eyes were damp.

"She has," she said. "She says he has something broken inside. He must not move around as he does if he is to live. But he is a stubborn man and will not listen to me. I do not know what to do."

Ma reached over and laid her hand on Long Star's arm. "Zeb will speak with Two Hand," she said.

Long Star looked at Pa. "If only you can get him to listen."

Me and Henry had come in and were standing by the fire warming our backsides. As I listened to the adult's conversation, Henry was eyeing the bearskin placed over Two Hand. Who could blame him? There weren't many folks in them mountains had ever seen such a hide.

Pa looked over and noticed that we had come in. Lookin' to get Long Star's mind off Two Hand, he said, "Billy, when ya get warmed up a bit run out and fitch whatcha brought for Long Star."

"You got it Pa," I said. "I'm plenty warm now."

I was excited to show Long Star her new hinny, especially with Pa sayin' I brought it to her. I didn't quite know how he figured that, but I was mighty pleased he did.

I ran out the door with Henry right behind me.

"What's this all about?" asked Henry.

"Well, remember when I said you was gonna learn all about hinnies," I shouted as we ran. "This'n here is for your Ma. And you are gonna get to take care of it."

Henry laughed at first, then it struck him. The way I was grinnin' could only mean one thing. I was tickled to be givin' another one of my chores to him. Taken care of a hinny.

"And whose idea might this've been?" he asked.

"Well, Pa come up with the hinny," I said. "But it may have been me who figured you and your ma could sure use it. And seein's how you're takin' care of a goat anyway, why a hinny wouldn't be no bother at all."

"Come to that outta the kindness of your heart, did ya?" said Henry. He then laughed and popped me on the back of my head.

"Well, it's mighty good of your pa anyway. No matter what your reasons were. It'll come in real handy for Ma gettin' around."

In no time at all we had the hinny unhobbled and brought her up to the cabin where Ma, Pa, and Long Star, all stood waiting.

"Billy figured you could use a sure-footed animal to get you around out here," Pa said to Long Star.

"This here is a hinny. She's got the straighter hoofs and powerful legs of a mule so she'll get ya where no horse ever could. And she can live on about any graze you put her on, so you won't hafta waste your corn on her. She's got a real smooth gait, an even temperament, and she won't spook near as quick as a horse. All in all, she's one fine mountain critter. 'Bout the only thing she won't do is work. Some folks think hinnies are too stubborn. I reckon they just might be too smart."

"She's wonderful," Long Star said as she looked the little hinny over.

I don't reckon she saw any fault in the breed. The horse head with oversized ears, the short stature with massive legs, the thick, full mane, the tail of a horse on a donkey body. To Long Star she was beautiful.

"I don't know what to say," said Long Star. "You have all been so good to me."

She looked at Ma and Pa as she brushed her hand over the hinny's thick winter coat.

Ma was hugging Pa and smiling.

"And she comes with a saddle and tack," Pa said.

"Oh, thank you, thank you all," she said.

"No need to thank us," said Pa. "It was Billy here that figured you'd have the best use for her."

She rushed over and hugged me, and kissed me on the cheek

"Thank you, Billy," she said. "I love her."

"Aw shucks," I said, as I rubbed my cheek and felt my ears heatin' up. "It weren't nothin'."

Everyone laughed at that, then Me and Henry took the hinny back out to the clearing with the mules as Long Star and Ma went back in and started fixing our midday meal.

The rest of the day was spent catchin' up on all the things that had happened in the Cove, and at Black Gum Shoal.

Pa gave Long Star and Henry a more detailed version of the bear fight; how Two Hand had once again saved his life by jumping on the bear's back and fighting it hand to hand.

Everyone looked at the massive bearskin that now covered Two Hand and marveled that the old man could have survived such an ordeal.

He then told them about taking the bearskin to show the Cobbs that the beast was dead, and about meeting up with Diver's kin on the way home.

Ma couldn't help but describe Clive and his ways to Long Star. The two of them had to muffle their laughter to keep from waking Two Hand.

Pa then told Diver's story and how he came to be at the waterfall were Pa saved him from the pool.

When Pa was done, Long Star told of the ordeal Two Hand had suffered since Pa had left him there.

Ahyoka had been guarded but optimistic that Two Hand would pull through. She said he was a powerful shaman and had a strong life force. If it was possible for a man to survive, Two Hand would do it.

For days it was iffy. He'd wake and seem better, then lapse into a coma-like-state and his breath would become shallow and ragged. He'd linger like that for hours and would become drenched with sweat.

Then one night he began gagging and Long Star helped him turn on his side where he spit up a large clout of tissue and blood with a sliver of bone in it.

Long Star sent Henry for Ahyoka.

When the medicine woman saw the mass and squeezed the bone between her fingers she nodded and had Long Star help her prop Two Hand up on her and Henry's pillows.

"It is a piece of rib bone, Ahyoka said. When the bear raked Two Hand's chest, he broke three ribs, smashing one and driving a sliver into his lung. If Two Hand had not coughed it out, he would have surely died. Now he must lie still until the puncture heals. He may recover, she said. Lung wounds often heal. But she warned I should be prepared for the worst."

"I will speak with him when he awakens," said Pa. "He will listen, or I'll tie him down."

"You speak mighty big for a greenhorn," they heard Two Hand say in a weak, shaky voice.

They all looked at the bed. Two Hand laid there watchin' them with his piercing, coal-black eyes. None of them had realized he was awake.

"How long have you been awake?" Pa said as he rose and walked over to Two Hand, placing a hand onto his forehead.

"Long enough to hear you say you are man enough to tie me down."

Pa grinned. "Well, under normal circumstances, I wouldn't want to try it, but I reckon the bear evened the odds a might. I figure I could take ya right now if you didn't put up too much of a fight."

Two Hand started to sit up, then sank back to his pillow. "I reckon you might be right," he said with a grimace.

"I'll do as Long Star says." He smiled. "Save me the effort of puttin' ya in your place."

"I'm mighty pleased to hear that," said Pa. "I was beginnin' to think my mouth had boasted of more than my gumption could handle."

Two Hand laid his head back and closed his eyes.

Pa looked at Long Star and she mouthed, "Thank You."

Pa looked over at Henry and asked, "So what you been up to?"

Henry straightened up a bit like he always did when addressing an elder. "I just been tryin' to help out while Ma is nursin' Two Hand," said Henry.

"And doing a fine job of it," said Long Star.

"That's good," said Pa.

Henry nodded. "And now I reckon I'll be makin' that log shed by the brook a bit bigger to fit the hinny," he continued.

"Turnin' it into a stable are ya?" asked Pa.

"Yeah, we've had us a pack o' wolves hangin' 'round lately. They stay clear of the cabin in the daytime but come in closer at night, so I been lockin' up the goat in that old shed before dark. I don't reckon it's big enough for both animals in the long term, so I'm gonna make it bigger."

"Reckon it'll do 'em both for tonight?" asked Pa.

"Yeah, I reckon so," said Henry. "But that'll leave your mules unprotected."

"We'll bring them mules down in front of the cabin tonight," said Pa. "If any wolves come after 'em, they'll protect themselves 'til I can get to 'em. They's true mountain stock and know their hooves is for more than just walkin'. Then come tomorrow, me and Billy will help you build that stable."

"Well, I sure appreciate that," Henry said.

Henry and me spent the rest of the day leading Joleen and Gabby through the nearby forest gathering long, straight, fallen, tree trunks to use in the construction of Henry's stable. With the mules to drag the timbers to the worksite, it was an easy task.

At one point, while we were tying a nice pine log to Joleen's pull rope, I stopped Henry.

"There's something I've always wondered," I said.

"What's that," asked Henry.

"We've often talked about Two Hand. Is he truly a shapeshifter, or ageless, or Stoneman the liver eater?"

"I don't know." said Henry.

"Well, he seems to be around an awful lot when you and your Ma need him. Why, he's even laid-up in your house right now. Are you sayin' you don't know what he is?"

"Yeah. I was told as a young child to never question the ways of Two Hand," Henry said.

"He protects many people in need. But he can also be fierce. If he would turn on me when he changes, I don't know. But Ma trusts him."

Henry then looked me in the face and said, "He's a close friend of your pa too. Did you ever ask your pa about him?"

I scratched my head. "I surly never have," I said. "Ain't that somethin'?"

By late afternoon we figured we had plenty of logs, so after takin' the mules to the brook to drink we tied them off to a stake near the cabin's front door on long lead lines. Any commotion would be heard from the house and Pa could deal with it from the doorway.

I was kinda lookin' forward to a wolf pelt or two come mornin'.

We then took a pail and milked the goat. To my surprise she was about to have kids. Henry said they had a distant neighbor with goats, and they'd visited with them a time or two. Now their goat gift would become even more generous. A goat usually has between one and three kids. By the size of this one, I would guess it was gonna be three.

Henry said Long Star had already named the goat, Usdi E tsi, or Little Mother.

I figured that was a real fine name.

"How 'bout the hinny?" I asked.

"She said your Pa made a crack about its bein' a Jenny hinny, so that's what she named it, Jenny."

After we were done milking, we locked the goat and Jenny in the shed and took the milk to Long Star. She strained it through flax linen, then set aside a large cup of it for Two Hand and after covering the rest, set it outside to cool.

It was a pleasant evening and we all joined in telling stories and discussing local events that could affect our lives. We enjoyed a good meal of elk stew, flatbread, and cool goat's milk.

Two Hand awoke from time to time and Long Star helped him sit up to eat a bit of stew in warm goat's milk. She gave him a little boneset and peppermint tea, to help in the healing process and to settle his coughing fits.

Pa cleaned and loaded his Hawkins and set it near the door, ready to settle the score with any four-legged varmints that might want to harm his stock.

Finally, about nine o'clock or so we all turned in for the night, Ma and Pa in Henry's bed, Long Star in a chair near Two Hand, and me and Henry on the floor near the fireplace.

Other than the occasional coughing fit from Two Hand, it was a quiet night.

The wolves were either too cowardly to try and challenge the mules so close to the cabin, or they had found easier pursuits elsewhere.

I did hear the far off howl of a wolf sometime in the early hours, but nothing nearby. Come morning Pa's rifle had been unfired.

TWENTY-TWO

Welcome News

T HE NEXT MORNING, we began work on Henry's stable.

After trimming the dead limbs from the logs we'd gathered, we used flat stones to form foundation corners twelve feet out from the east wall of the shack. After that, it was a simple job of sliding the logs into the gaps between the existing wall timbers then notching and placing cross timbers to form the new east wall. Pa then used a broad axe to cut out a large section of the original wall to open the two rooms into one.

A strong center beam was placed midway of the new enclosure and the whole room was topped with a couple dozen straight saplings supporting a sod roof interlaced by long grass roots.

Finally, the log sections that were cut out of the old wall were used to fill the gap below the bottom timbers. This was all reinforced with fieldstones in such a way as to prevent hungry predators from burrowing beneath the wall.

By mid-afternoon, the stable was complete and strong enough to withstand anything the denizens of the forest could throw at it. The walls were sturdy, the sod-roof raintight, and the entire structure had more than enough room for Jenny, Little Mother, and the kids that would soon be arriving.

"A fine job," Pa said as he gave the stable a last inspection. "You get the gumption some time, you might want to chalk the north and west walls to cut the wind. Other than that, your critters outta feel right at home," Pa told Henry.

"Yeah, I'll sure do that, Mr. Banion," said Henry. "And I can't thank y'all enough for the help."

"Don't mention it," said Pa. "Happy to do it."

Two Hand had slept most of the day, according to Ma and Long Star, and seemed a bit stronger by suppertime that evening. The coughin' fits had become less frequent and not near as violent.

I reckon gettin' that bone sliver outta his lungs had helped.

His mood had also improved. He asked after Diver, as he ate more soft food and drank the boneset tea that Long Star gave him. He remembered his word to Pa and did what Long Star asked of him without complaint.

He nodded his approval upon learning that Diver had recovered from his malady and had returned to his wife.

"This is good," he said. "A man needs to know his past, his truth. To stand by his works or correct his failings. I wish him well. He is a good man. Now, I will sleep."

After supper, Ma insisted that Long Star get some sleep on Henry's mat. She knew that Long Star would spend another long night sitting next to Two Hand and assured her that she would be waked up before her and Pa went to bed.

Me and Henry had already milked Little Mother and placed her and Jenny in the barn, making sure the door was latched tight. We then went out to the clearing where we had left the mules in the thick grass and brought them around front where they could be watched over.

We then brought in firewood, fetched a bucket of water from the brook, in case Long Star needed it overnight, and hauled the days food scraps well down stream before throwing them in the water. Henry said that was one of his daily chores to help keep wild predators from being drawn to their cabin.

Back home, we fed our scraps to the pigs.

After a long day, come nine-thirty or so, me and Henry once again went to sleep in front of the fire

It was a cold night. Pa replenished the fire twice. Sometime in the early hours, Two Hand was once again racked by coughing fits. I don't reckon any of us got much sleep after that.

By first light we were all up and Ma was making breakfast. Me and Henry went out and milked the goat and turned her and Jenny out. The wolves had once again been a no-show.

I was a bit concerned that Jenny might stray without hobbles, but Henry said the goat always ran free in the daytime and as we watched Jenny stayed near her. I guess they bonded overnight, so we let them roam. Henry said if she did stray, he would find her well before dark and return her to the barn.

Ahyoka showed up around noon to check up on Two Hand. Pa was impressed, remembering how Kendree couldn't be bothered with a patient once he'd done his damage.

Long Star told Ahyoka, Two Hand had done quite well the previous evening but had a hard night.

Ahyoka nodded. "Lung wounds take time," she said as she felt his head. "He is warm but not in danger."

She then had Pa help him sit up so she could unwrap the bandage from his barrel chest and remove the poultice Long Star had placed the day before.

"Good," she said as she gently probed the wound.

It must have hurt something fierce, but Two Hand, made not a sound.

"The poison is small and there are no bubbles in the blood. A few more days and he will be past the worst of it."

She then turned to Pa. "You stay or you go?"

"We need to be getting home, but we'll stay as long as we are needed," he said.

"Hmm," said Ahyoka. "You stay until tomorrow, then I will return. My daughter will help. Long Star will not be alone."

She then prepared another poultice and rewrapped Two Hand.

As she left, she honored Pa with a blessing.

"Let the Great One watch over you Zebulon Banion and all who you cherish."

"Thank you, Agitsi (Mother)," he said.

At Long Star's request, Henry had been busy saddling Jenny. When Ahyoka came out he told her to take the hinny. She could bring her back when she returned.

Ahyoka smiled. She had always loved donkeys but had not ridden one in many years.

"I thank you, Henry," she said. "I will be here early."

We had all gathered at the door as she rode away and couldn't help but smile. She rode with stiff legs in the stirrups sticking out to the sides and she was just a cackling like an old, spotted hen. The reins were held about head high in one hand and she had the other hand wrapped tight in Jenny's thick mane, as if in fear of falling off. As short as that hinny was, she couldn't have fell far, but I guess she didn't wanna risk it.

I don't know what Jenny thought about the whole thing, but Ahyoka was loving it.

We spent one last night at Long Star's cabin. Pa sat and talked with Two Hand until he fell asleep and then made sure the old man was tucked in tight. It was another bitter cold night, perhaps the coldest of the year, and snow fell leaving a couple of inches.

Thankfully, Two Hand had a better night and only woke up coughing a few times. Long Star gave him a sip of peppermint tea and he drifted right off.

True to her word, Ahyoka arrived around eight the following morning.

Me and Henry went out and eased the half-frozen medicine woman off Jenny and helped her into the house. Ma helped her out of her fox lined coat and sat her in front of the fireplace.

She had been riding straight into an easterly wind the entire way from her holdings in North Carolina and was fortunate she didn't suffer frostbite.

Ma packed our things as I helped Henry do his morning chores. Luckily, the winds died down and the bitterness eased.

Pa said his farewells to Two Hand and said he would check on him again as soon as he could. Two Hand tried to get Pa to take back the bearskin, but Pa said it belonged to the warrior who fought it hand to hand. He said Long Star was going to fashion it into a great robe to replace that old tattered grizzly half-hide that Two Hand often wore.

By nine-thirty we were on our way.

With the calming of the winds the temperatures rose, and it was a beautiful morning. Pa, along with his ever-present Hawkins, rode Joleen. Ma rode behind me on Gabby.

For quite some time no one spoke. It somehow seemed irreverent to disturb the solitude of the quiet, glistening forest.

Then around eleven in the morning it began to snow. At first it was just the occasional small flake settling on an eyelash or on the manes of the mules.

It was easy to assume a gentle breeze had whisked the tiny crystal from an overhead limb and it settled upon us as we passed below.

Then gradually, the air thickened with flakes. First dime size, then half-dollar size, and finally as big as the palms of Pa's hands.

It was a beautiful sight, no denying that, but we knew it would get deeper and make traveling harder, so, we stepped up the pace of the mules. They seemed to understand the urgency and gave us no trouble. Within forty-five minutes the mountain clearings were covered in a banket of snow that reached above the mule's knees. On occasion Pa's deerskin boots drug great furrows in the white powder on each side of Joleen's flanks.

Pa led us through the deep woods where the forest canopy kept much of the snow from reachin' the ground below. Pa knew of every hill, every crag, and every other feature in them mountains. He knew how to avoid the bald knobs, the valley meadows, and the steep ridge descents. But to tell you the truth, I was still gettin' a bit concerned. I'd heard tales of folks gettin' snowed in deep in the back county and havin' to sit it out for several days before it lifted. Even heard tell of one or two freezin' to death.

However, we kept at it, and long about one-thirty or two in the afternoon, Pa led us 'round a big ol' blown-down and we came out into the pine corps below Pa and Diver's cornfield. We'd made it to the homestead, and a half hour later we rode up to the front porch. During the entire ride, it had not stopped snowing.

"Hello. Good to have y'all back." We turned toward the shed and saw Pat workin' his way toward us through the deep snow. As he drew near, he reached out and shook Pa's hand.

"Glad y'all made it. I was beginnin' to think I's gonna be up here for the next week or so, the way this snow's been a fallin'"

"I'm glad we made it too," said Pa. "I can't thank you enough for watchin' the place."

"Don't mention it," said Pat. "Here, let me take your mules. Y'all gotta be half frozen after that ride. Go on in and get warmed up. I'll take care of them." He took the reins and waited while we climbed down.

"Then I reckon I'll head on down the hill while I still can."

Pa took Ma's arm and nodded to Pat.

"Well, I thank you again," he said. "And tell your Pa, I'll be down to see him when I can."

"I'll do that, Mr. Banion," Pat said. "Y'all take care now." With that Pat led the mules toward the barn and we went inside. Pa built up a warm fire and Ma put some coffee on to warm our innards.

A half hour or so later, Pa looked out and saw Pat ride by on his own mule. The snow was rubbin' the mule's belly, but Pa didn't figure they'd have much trouble gettin' down to Clarence's place. Pa waved and Pat waved back.

It snowed for the next two days. Luckily, it wasn't them big palm sized flakes, more like nickel sized, but it still made a mighty deep bank to be pushin' through.

We didn't make it off that mountain 'til late January and no one could make it up either.

We had plenty of hay stored above the stock room in the barn for the animals, so that wasn't a concern. But we did have to create a path so the cow and mules could make it down to the creek to drink. I had water enough to haul for the pigs, the chickens, and our needs. I sure weren't lookin' to be haulin' it for the big stock.

Luckily, our stream was swift enough flowing that other than a swath along each bank, it didn't freeze.

The chickens had quit layin' but still had to be fed and watered. One day while I was chippin' ice off the coop latch to fill their feed trough and water bowl, I noticed scratch marks on the door and on a corner of the nesting box. Somethin' was tryin' to dig its way in.

I set traps and them critters must a been real hungry 'cause over the next week or so, I caught two weasels and a skunk.

Still, something was tryin' to get at them chickens.

As the snow settled and I got a better look at the tracks the critter left, I could make out it was a fox.

There ain't nothin' more wily than a fox.

I set trap after trap, but he always got around them. Luckily, that coop was built too strong for him to get in, but he wasn't givin' up either.

Finally, I came up with a plan I figured couldn't fail. I reenforced the nesting boxes and placed all the chickens in there where nothing could get to them. Then I loosened a board on the coop so the fox could break-in. Above the entrance spot, I fixed a trap door. When the fox broke in and tried to get into the nesting box, the door would close preventing his escape. The chickens would be safe, and the fox would be stuck inside the coop.

The next mornin', I rushed out anxious to see how my trap had worked.

No fox.

Upon closer inspection, I could see where the fox had pulled back the loose board and entered the coop. He had indeed tried to get into the nesting box and caused the trap door to set. But then, he had somehow squeezed his body into a small opening between the door and the wall opening the trap and escaping.

My plan had worked, but the would-be thief got away anyway. At least, I reckon, it gave him a good scare, 'cause the rest of that winter I never had trouble with that fox again.

When the snow finally melted enough for the Cove trail to be used, Forrest showed up.

"How ya fairin' up here?" he asked Pa.

"Ain't complainin' none," said Pa. "Been kinda pleasant."

"Well, I got some news for ya from the Cove," said Forrest. "Seems that Pastor Wilson's pa passed away."

"Sorry to hear it," said Pa.

"Yeah, he was some shook up about it hisself. He come by my place and asked if I'd ride up here with him. Said he had something to discuss with ya."

Pa nodded.

"When we got here, we met up with Pat. He said y'all had gone to Long Star's place and didn't know when you'd be back."

"That's so," said Pa.

"So, anyway, he said he had to go to Trenton, New Jersey to settle his Pa's affairs," continued Forrest. "Figured he may not be back 'til mid-summer, maybe not 'til next fall. Never did say what he was needin' to discuss with you."

Pa scratched his bearded chin. "I can't imagine," he said.

"Well anyway, it was a big rush. Him and Mary just got out o' here a couple days before the big snow. With that nice rig he has, I reckon they cleared the mountains fine.

"Then, yesterday, I received a letter for you," Forrest said as he pulled a letter from his coat pocket and handed it to Pa. "It's addressed from Diver."

Pa stared at the letter as if he didn't know what to do with it.

"Let's take it in so your Ma can share the news."

When Pa and Forrest entered the dining room, Ma was rollin' out pie dough as I told her tales 'bout Lancelot and Sir Gawain and all them other knights that sat at King Arthur's round table. We was both so involved in the legends that we didn't even notice Pa 'til he said he had some news for us.

"Sit down," he told me and Ma. "You'll want to hear this."

We all four sat at the kitchen table after Ma fetched some coffee for Pa and Forrest, and some sassafras tea for herself and me.

"Forrest brought some news from the Cove," Pa said. He then told us Pastor Wilson's pa had died and the pastor and Mary were on their way to New Jersey.

They were gonna be gone the whole summer? I gotta say, I was a bit devastated.

Ma understood what I was a feelin' and reached over to squeeze my hand.

Pa then placed the letter on the table in front of us. "And this," he said, "is from Diver."

We sat transfixed.

"Well, open it," said Ma.

Pa smiled at Ma's impatience, then reached down and broke the small, wax, seal holding the letter shut. He spread it out on the table.

He read. "Dear Kate, Zeb and Billy. We made it home fine. Hope you are all doing well. I received a visit today from Pastor Wilson and Mary. He has been called away on personal business and asked if I could watch over his flock while he is away. Charlotte wishes to see where I spent last year and to meet all of you. We will arrive soon. Wilson offered his house, but we would prefer our own. Perhaps we could use my old room until we find one. See you soon. Homer 'Diver' McCoy."

"Wee!" squealed Ma. "Diver's comin' home."

We all laughed. Even the news that Mary would be gone for several months couldn't dampen the joy I felt that Diver was comin' back. He had been a major influence in my life, and I'll tell ya, that wasn't gonna change.

If I'd only known what was comin' next time Diver arrived at our home in the mist.

Epilogue

WELL THAT'S ABOUT ALL I GOTTA SAY for today. I hope y'all enjoyed it as much as I enjoyed tellin' it. Y'all come on back again iffen' you want to know 'bout what happened after Diver come home. There's still a heap o' story to tell about that.

Then there's a mess a story 'bout ol' Two Hand ya ain't heard yet either. And 'bout Ma, Pa, Henry, Second Chance, Mary, Forrest and all the folks down yonder in the Cove.

Now, y'all take care and be safe on your journey home. Steer clear of that chicken house down yonder. That ol' rooster takes some after his granddaddy, 'ceptin' he hates everybody! Heehee.

Well, y'all come back when ya take the notion, ya hear?

Bye now.

Be sure to be lookin' for
Billy and your other favorite
characters from
Cades Cove to return in . . .

A HOME IN THE MIST III

WILDERNESS JOURNEY

Out now

Please leave a review on Amazon if you liked
this book.
I thank you kindly.